MW01199521

BY ED PARK

Personal Days

Same Bed Different Dreams

An Oral History of Atlantis

AN ORAL HISTORY OF ATLANTIS

An

ORAL HISTORY

of

ATLANTIS

STORIES

ED PARK

RANDOM HOUSE
New York

Random House
An imprint and division of Penguin Random House LLC
1745 Broadway, New York, NY 10019
randomhousebooks.com
penguinrandomhouse.com

Published in the United States by Random House, an imprint and division of Penguin Random House LLC, New York.

RANDOM HOUSE and the HOUSE colophon are registered trademarks of Penguin Random House LLC.

Parts of this book have appeared in *The New Yorker* ("The Wife on Ambien," "Slide to Unlock"), *McSweeney's* ("The Air as Air"), *The Baffler* ("Machine City"), *Open City* ("Bring on the Dancing Horses"), *Trampoline: An Anthology* ("Well-Moistened with Cheap Wine . . ."), *Columbia Magazine* ("Two Laptops"), *Pioneer Works Broadcast* ("Seven Women"), *Vice* ("Thought and Memory"), *Columbia: A Journal of Arts and Letters* ("An Oral History of Atlantis"), *The 2024 Short Story Advent Calendar* ("Eat Pray Click"), and *Virgin Fiction* ("A Note to My Translator"). "Weird Menace" was released as an Audible Original.

Hardcover ISBN 9780812998993
Ebook ISBN 9780812988338

Printed in the United States of America on acid-free paper

randomhousebooks.com

1 3 5 7 9 8 6 4 2

First Edition

Book design by Fritz Metsch

The authorized representative in the EU for product safety and compliance is Penguin Random House Ireland, Morrison Chambers, 32 Nassau Street, Dublin D02 YH68, Ireland. https://eu-contact.penguin.ie.

For Duncan, Keeler, and Sandra

For somehow we know by instinct that outsize buildings cast the shadow of their own destruction before them, and are designed from the first with an eye to their later existence as ruins.

—W. G. Sebald, *Austerlitz*

CONTENTS

AN ORAL HISTORY OF ATLANTIS

A NOTE TO MY TRANSLATOR

Dear E.,

Thank you for your letter. We are doing well here, relaxing as best we can, but a few of your queries anent the ongoing translation of *Mexican Fruitcake* (as you insist on rendering the title) disturb me profoundly. Time prevents me from undertaking my own Englishing of the thing, and since you had been recommended by a (once-) trusted friend, I agreed to have you do the deed. I understand that "French" is an obscure and obsolete tongue, but we must have something like standards, yes? To go along with some of your suggestions (not to mention your outright, brazen, unnoted blunders) would be akin to an automobile manufacturer issuing cars with only one tire, and that one deflated, and no brakes to speak of. To wit:

Page one: The novel begins with a hailing of the muse and a quick history of man's moral awakening, mastery of his surroundings, and subsequent fall from grace. In my version. In *your* version, a man named Mr. Henry enters a flat in London and discovers that his wife is taking stomach medication. You go on to say that it is raining outside and that an oblong (?) Quaker youth is on a "hickey spree." I respectfully suggest you put aside whatever hallucinogens you might be keeping on your nightstand and concentrate on the text I have provided you with.

Page two: Why "knickers"? Wherefore "fugitive uranium"? Why not call a spade a spade—or, as the case may be, a rubbery bathtub ornament a rubbery bathtub ornament?

Page seven: Who is Solomon Eveready? What is he doing in my book?

Page eight: You asked, in your letter, what sort of chess pieces I had in mind when I wrote this scene. Were they carved of wood, you asked, or ivory, or were they simply molded from plastic? I cannot answer this question for you, E., since there are no chess sets (and hence no chess pieces) in the meticulously researched milieu of my novel—that milieu being the incredibly serious, hands-pressed-in-a-gesture-of-prayer inner world of a man who sits alone and dundrearied off the coast of Madagascar.

To add insult to injury, you hint that the novel might be strengthened if you—you, my translator!—"quietly added some minor details," such as "half a page or so" (kindly submitted for my inspection) in which you identify the chess pieces one by one, explaining how the tall one that bears the likeness of General Grant is the king of the "Union" side, how the eight men with bugles are pawns, etc. Even if I were to do the unthinkable and allow you to mention a chess set resting on my delicate "open-leafed end table" (or, as you have it, "dog"), why in God's name would you make it a Civil War chess set? And why are the pieces arranged in such a way that, when viewed sideways, they spell the word "GOLFNUT"?

Page eight, a little lower down: The doctrine of transubstantiation has nothing to do with pinball.

Page nine: Solomon Eveready reappears, this time smoking cut-grade reefer and imitating a trout. Explain this to me. Explain also the presence of scuba gear that "reeks of melon."

Page ten: Only ten pages into my novel and already all seems lost. I no longer recognize characters, points of plot, dialogue. I frankly have no idea what the words before me mean. Here you present a heated argument between two nuns (and are they truly *robot* nuns?), both of whom speak a weird amalgam of Cantonese and the International Morse Code. Can you help me? Please?

≈

So ends my criticism of the first chapter of your version of my novel. I have neglected, for brevity's sake, to note all the boners that litter every page of your rendition—solecisms that would be hilarious were not the matter at hand of such obvious importance. I am an unknown commodity in America; this is the book that will either build my stateside reputation or consign me evermore to the coldest remainder bin at the local Price Club. The minute I receive your letter indicating that you were pulling my leg, as they say, I will laugh and benignly destroy *my* letter to my American publisher, in which I go into excruciating detail about my proficiency in the deadly Brazilian martial art known as capoeira, and the stylish havoc I have been known to wreak.

Until then,
I am,
Hans de Krap

BRING ON THE DANCING HORSES

WHEN I CALL my parents, my mom tells me my dad is busy teaching a class on the internet. That is, the class is in a classroom but the topic is the internet. More specifically, he's teaching seniors—that is, old people—how to blog, write anonymous comments on news articles without panicking, poke their children on Facebook, and get away with not writing h, t, t, p, colon, forward slash, forward slash, w, w, w, dot before every web address.

I had no idea my dad liked the internet so much. "Who said anything about like?" my mom says. I can hear her clicking away at her keyboard in the background.

My dad is retired—or was. Is it that they need the money? I fantasize about a heretofore unknown gambling problem, hush funds, love children. My mom sells my old comic books and De La Soul cassingles on eBay. She doesn't know I know. Every so often I'll think about stuff I loved in my youth, and a search inevitably brings up her dealer name.

I amp the bidding when it seems safe. You could say I'm looking out for her. But how is it that her four grown kids have neglected their parents' financial needs?

I go to bed with a nagging sense of guilt, though this is how I usually go to bed.

≈

My girlfriend, Tabby, reviews science fiction for a living, which just goes to show you that America is still the greatest, most useless country in the world.

She went to Penumbra College in Vermont and is ABD in comparative literature at Rue University. She's been ABD ever since we met, back when I didn't know what it stood for. Her dissertation is about one or possibly all of these things: manservant literature, robot literature, and the literature of deception.

Tabby is considerably older than me, and by considerably I mean over ten years. I told my parents five, but I don't think they believed me. Tabitha Grammaticus remembers not only life before the internet, but life before the affordable and relatively silent electric typewriter.

She reads fast, writes faster. She does monthly columns for the *California Science Fiction Review, Exoplanets* magazine, and the website for the Northwest Airlines' Frequent Flier Book Club, which is getting a soft launch.

≈

I didn't think it was possible for someone to read as fast as Tabby does, and for a long time I assumed she was a skimmer. But whenever I'd quiz her on a novel that we'd both read, she knew every detail. I'd sit there with the book open and ask things like: "Who answers the door in the middle of chapter 7?"

I tried to keep up with Tabby's reviewing, but it's hard when someone's so prolific. I am not friends with many writers, mostly because that means having to read all their articles, stories, essays, books, and even poetry. They expect you to have read it all. With Tabby, I tried. I really did.

But she's what she calls a stylist. I gave up on her *Exoplanets* column after the third one. I got stuck on the opening line: "All time travel is essentially Oedipal."

Tabby is a brilliant genius in her own way, but sometimes I worry that she is turning into an alien. Lately we don't go out much, and she has taken to wearing what she calls a housecoat about the house. Whenever I'd come across the word "housecoat" in a brittle British novel of misaddressed correspondence and quiet adultery, I would try to picture what was meant. I was never sure, but surely it isn't this thing that Tabby more or less lives in, a sort of down-filled poncho with stirrups.

≈

At the same time I'm attracted to this girl at work. I don't even want to know how old she is. My guess is that she's younger than me by a margin nearly as great as that separating me from Tabby. But what do I know about age? I thought Tabby was my age when I met her. I'm not a good judge of these things, possibly of anything.

The girl at work. I think English is her second language or possibly her third. She has a lisp and does crazy things with her hair. Her name is Deletia. I think it's the most beautiful name in the world.

Here's a secret. I wrote that down on a Post-it once—*You have the most beautiful name in the world*—and carried it stuck to the inside of a folder. All day I was hideously excited as I sat at my desk, roamed the corridors. Then I forgot about the note for a week. When I saw it again the words looked strange, like someone else had written them. Before throwing it away, I used the sticky edge to clean out the crevices of my keyboard.

≈

I have two older brothers, whom I despise, and a younger sister, whom I adore. My brothers have always been exceedingly nice to me, including me in all manner of conversation and sport, yet I can't stand the sight of them. At least individually. When the three of us sons are together, my ill will dissipates somewhat, into a tan-colored mist of indifference. My sister, Grace, on the other hand, speaks sharply to me and expects me to do things like pick up her dry cleaning and find her cheap tickets to Cancún on the internet. I mean the real Cancún, not some virtual *playa*. But she's the baby of the family and I'm happy to oblige.

We children all live in the city, and gatherings are complicated for me. If it's me, my eldest brother, Dan, and my sister, I get argumentative the second I walk in, under the impression that he is picking on her, being the bully that he undoubtedly is. If it's me, my other brother, and my sister, I'll tell jokes nonstop, poorly thought-out jokes that hinge on antiquated wordplay. I'm trying to defuse the tension caused by the fact that this brother is a withholding control freak.

In fact, my brothers are exceedingly nice to my sister as well, and she does not speak sharply to them or expect them to run her errands. Sometimes I think she respects them because they make money and I don't, really. Or because their wives are elegant, capable women, and Tabby is something of an eccentric and a bit of a slob.

Once I was on a bus going crosstown and saw Grace and my brothers walking out of a restaurant, laughing. They looked gloriously happy. Dan posted a picture of their lunch on Facebook. I don't know what he was thinking.

≈

After internet class, my dad emails. His spelling, in flowing longhand, has always been impeccable, but something about email makes him spell like Prince. I often have to read his messages aloud, pronouncing the letters and numbers until I figure out the meaning.

I email back and ask if he wants to chat online. No response, though I know he's still awake. He keeps updating his Facebook posts. Doesn't he know I can see them? Doesn't he know I'm his friend? I stay up till two watching his wording get terse.

≈

Every day, sometimes more than once, science-fiction books arrive at the door by mail or messenger. Tabby tears into them. Slabs of space opera line the hall, mortared with mindbenders in which the Union loses or Hitler is an android.

There's this one FedEx guy who drops by a couple times a week, bearing such goodies. He's practically family at this point. He buzzes from the lobby three times, insistently, like he's doing an *O* in Morse code. Tabby hits the door button without asking who it is.

The FedEx guy looks, she once said, like an underwear model with clothes on. Of course Tabby's not attracted to FedEx, as she's easily twice his age. But you can never be sure. They always make a suspicious amount of small talk. Today she tells me that he's an aspiring writer and wants her advice on where to send stories.

"Are they even science fiction?" I ask.

"They're *speculative* fiction," she says. FedEx has given her some of his work, and apparently it's pretty good, a self-conscious throwback to the age of the pulps, with a slick commercial veneer. She's thinking of writing a column about him.

"But he hasn't published anything yet," I say.

"Oh he will, and he has," she says, like someone well acquainted with time travel.

≈

I never told my siblings that I saw them from the bus, though I put up a cryptic post on my secret blog. "Sometimes the people you think you can depend on turn out to be *not* so dependable," I wrote. No one knows I have the blog. I've had it for two years but in my mind I've had it for longer, from even before there was something called the internet. It averages three readers a week, people not named me. I keep meaning to delete the thing, but the required authentications have changed so much that I can't even figure out how to do it.

Maybe my dad could help me. Lately I've been wondering if he can do my sister's internet chores for her, like get those plane tickets or update her Facebook status. Grace hasn't logged on to Facebook in a long time. I know this because I keep getting little messages in the corner: Reconnect with Grace. Write on her Wall.

≈

Something tells me Tabby will never finish her dissertation. Part of her wants to finish just to finish. She wants "PhD" after her name. But realistically, she's never going to teach. There are no jobs in robot literature or manservant literature. I don't know what the literature of deception is.

The latest twist is that Rue University no longer exists in the material sense. It became a low-residency institution two years ago, then an online-only entity, with all teaching, discussion, and advisement done via email. Now Rue's just a diploma mill. "It's not even worth the paper it's printed on," Tabby says cheerfully. The joke here is that they don't even send you a diploma, just a PDF that you can download and print if you like.

≈

Tabby gives me a book for my birthday. It's a review copy of something called *The Truculáta: A Tale of the Weëmim.* I thank her and we have sex. She keeps the poncho on, stirrups and all. Later I escape to the study with my gift. The prologue begins:

> Ten thousand years have passed since the S'rwrwa conquered the outer colonies of the Confederation, enslaving its peoples by means of superior firepower and the Naxx, a form of mass hypnosis perfected by the rogue wizards known as the Qmzic.

I glance at the cover art: a bowtie-shaped spaceship whirling into the void. I notice that *The Truculáta* is book two in the third of four projected trilogies—the entire sequence is dubbed The Last Chronicles of the Terraplex. I grit my teeth and read on.

> Only the mysterious Weëmim, a clan of psychics descended from the Grand Vizier Fungwafer VIII and his half-horse concubine, continues to offer resistance. But overwhelmed by the S'rwrwan robot army, and the rise of the vicious Lord Exanthatrill, the Weëmim are dying out.

Their only hope is to bribe the Qmzic with the mind-altering seaweed they harvest, and use their powers to unlock the secrets of a small "cube" of impossible geometries called . . . the Truculáta.

I'm forever reading about people who get so incensed at a book that they fling it across the room. This always seemed to me journalistic boilerplate, like those ten-minute standing ovations you read about at the Cannes Film Festival. Nevertheless, for the first time in my life, I fling a book across the room. The six-hundred-page bulk of *The Truculáta* leaves a dent in the wall, which I attempt to conceal by moving the lamp.

Later Tabby and her poncho glide into the study. She picks up *The Truculáta,* moves the lamp back into position, and begins underlining passages of note.

≈

That evening Deletia sends me text messages that are either extremely suggestive or simply misspelled. I don't think Tabby would ever go through my BlackBerry, but who knows?

I delete the texts. I delete Deletia. She texts me again an hour later. It's the kind of message that makes my heart go out of control. I can't breathe. I write back, Is this you? No response. Then at three in the morning: YES HONEY.

As it turns out, a bunch of us got these saucy missives. At work the next day she explains that someone hacked her phone and email, that you should change your passwords every month. I can't tell if she's saying that the hacker is an ex-boyfriend or a criminal from her home country, or if these two shadowy figures are one and the same.

Later, when I'm supposed to be working on some numbers, I write her name on a Post-it, over and over again, a downpour of Deletia, and put it in my shirt pocket, right over my heart.

≈

For the past year, and without my knowledge, Tabby has been running a heroic fantasy website called Swords of Amber Mist.

"I didn't think you'd be interested," she explains.

I peek as she updates the site. It's largely fanfic, with characters from different books and movies interbreeding. Aliens, animals, *Homo sapiens*. This is what happens, in post after post. The copulation, as it's often called, takes place in caverns, on ancient battlefields, or in "antechambers." The background is a starlit black, undulating with digital smoke that rises from skull-shaped braziers.

You need to be over eighteen and a paying member to read or contribute to Swords of Amber Mist. There are banner ads for online role-playing games, medieval-sounding deodorant.

"Does FedEx write for this?" I ask.

"You mean Harris? He's on SoAM all the time," she says. "Oh, he stopped by while you were at the cleaners. There's a package for you in the hall."

≈

On the bench in the hall is one of those silky impermeable FedEx envelopes. The texture's like that of Tabby's futuristic poncho. It's from my mom—or, rather, her eBay avatar—and it's addressed to my username, which she has put in quotation marks. Somehow this kills me.

There's no note inside, no indication that she knows who I am. This is Tabby's address, not mine.

I pull out something sky blue, the cloth as thin as tissue in places. Then I get it: I've unwittingly won the auction for my old Echo and the Bunnymen T-shirt, from that show I didn't even go to. It was sort of after their heyday. I put in the bid two months ago and promptly forgot about it. On the back of the shirt it says: "Bring on the Dancing Horses."

THE WIFE ON AMBIEN

THE WIFE ON Ambien knows the score. I mean this literally. Rangers 4–3 in overtime. Devils fall to the Flames, 3–1. Knicks lose again at home. In the morning I open the paper and none of this checks out.

The wife on Ambien calls me Bob, calls me Mom, calls me Mr. Bluepants.

The wife on Ambien makes false starts. In one week alone she's sketched a music hall (she is not an architect), designed a drone (she is not an engineer), written two scenes of a play called *Haunted Masquerade* (her MFA is in sculpture). The handwriting is a bear, but I piece together a plot: society lady leads double life in the London of Jack the Ripper. In the morning the wife on Ambien denies authorship, though later at lunch I hear the first line of the soliloquy leave her lips.

The wife on Ambien cooks eggs. I take pains to hide the ingredients and the hardware. Still she conjures omelettes, from a secret stash of eggs, with a pan I somehow miss. She singes her robe. I gain five pounds in a month.

•

The wife on Ambien gets fresh. She moves on top of me like it's spin class. That was nice, I say afterward. Really nice. It reminds me of our wedding night. Paris! My God! We were so young! Do you remember how the stars, I say, and stop, because she's already snoring.

The wife on Ambien tries to order Ambien on Amazon.

The wife on Ambien makes up names of golfers.

The wife on Ambien has a clean conscience. You don't want to know what I did in Tucson, she says, patting me on the head, like a child. I'd better not say what went down in West Hartford. Tell me, I say. She looks around for some eggs.

The wife on Ambien shifts her legs. To the left, to the right, to the left, to the right. She bends and extends. What are you doing, I whisper in her ear. Skiing, she says. Skiing in the Canadian Rockies with Mr. Bluepants.

The wife on Ambien recites the poetry of T. S. Eliot, sings the music of the Jesus and Mary Chain, calculates how much we need to save to retire. Her figures vary. The wife on Ambien also tells me it doesn't matter, that the sun will swallow the earth exactly eight billion years, or thirteen weeks, or twenty-four hours from now.

The wife on Ambien hails Uber after Uber. The cars stream toward us like a series of sharks. It's four A.M. Drivers from many countries gather on the corner, fling curses at our window, break out the booze, promise each other their children in marriage.

The wife on Ambien hacks into my Facebook account and leaves slurs on the pages of my enemies. Get a life, you're a joke. She joins political causes directly opposed to her own. I spend an hour every morning cleaning up the digital trail.

The wife on Ambien shouts, Atlantis! Just that. *Atlantis!*

The wife on Ambien has been known to drink an entire pint of milk. She washes out the slim jug and stands it up like a soldier in the recycling bin.

The wife on Ambien forgets about our children, Danica, eleven, and Morris, five. We named them after a race-car driver and a cat. It was her idea. She had it on Ambien. I get home from work after nine and see them attacking each other with belts while she sleeps, all the cushions and pillows piled in the center of the living room. Don't wreck our fort, Daddy, Morris says. That's more like a tower, I say. Then don't wreck our tower, Danica says. What about homework? I ask. Homework's for losers, she says. Losers like you, says Morris. Honey, I call, but the wife on Ambien is sawing logs.

The wife on Ambien takes her vitamins, organizes the spice rack. She alphabetizes the shelves in the hallway and polishes my shoes. She wanders awhile, adjusting any picture frames out of true. Everything looks cleaner in the morning. But other nights she's knocking tchotchkes off tables, surrounding the wastebasket with coffee grounds in ritual fashion.

The wife on Ambien—how can I describe her? The way she tilts her head reminds me of pictures of her grandmother as a youth. The way she does a Bronx cheer reminds me of my first boss, who was in the Merchant Marine.

The wife on Ambien scrolls through her phone, swipes with her eyes shut. I can't wrench it from her iron grip. In the morning she says, Did you change the time zone to Dubai?

I sense a light. It's three-fifteen and the wife on Ambien is playing online poker. Around the virtual table one night are Joker17, AceInHole, and Mr_Bluepants. I would force her to stop, but she's winning by a lot. Someone has to bring home the bacon while my start-up starts up. That's how I figure it. I'm seeking funding for a virtual-reality venture that will let you live in the home you grew up in.

The wife on Ambien can list the presidents in order. The wife in real life can't.

The wife on Ambien tries her hand at painting. The tubes are open, the brushes stand in a coffee can of gray water, there's a becoming beige smudge on her brow, but where are the canvases, whither the tableaux? Many years later, when we move out of the city, I find her art under a box of books in the basement storage locker. These are all pictures of toast, I say.

•

The wife on Ambien solves Danica's Rubik's Cube.

The wife on Ambien insists she doesn't snore. One night I set up my phone to record her, balancing it on an eyeglass case between our pillows, wondering if it's legal. In the morning, the device tells a different tale. It's just me, calling out her name, my voice thinning to a whine, like a dog that's strayed too far from its master. A voice that could keep the best of us up at night.

MACHINE CITY

I'M NOT AN actor, but I was in a movie once. Bethany Blanket cast me as a painter in her student project, my sophomore year at Yale. In one scene, I was made up to look old: wrinkled brow, wig streaked white with talc. This morning, in the elevator at work, I saw that face again. Fun way to start the day.

Machine City was a half-hour two-hander. It screened the weekend before winter break, at an unheated auditorium in the law school. You could see your breath. *The Yale Herald* called our film "baffling" but doled out three and a half stars—grade inflation. Tickets were four bucks. Sixty people came to watch. I don't know where the money went.

I just searched for the movie online. No trace, thank God. Or is it better if the thing still lives? The internet barely existed when I was in college. Email was an impractical novelty. You'd send someone a message, and weeks might pass before they saw it. The message invariably ran something like *Hey, just saying hello on this crazy machine, have a nice day*. You could only check email at a handful of terminals sprinkled around campus. No one had a modem back then, and the phones had coiled cords.

Bethany Blanket and I crossed paths thanks to the god of student housing, a minor deity who put us on the third floor of Entryway D of Saybrook College, overlooking Elm Street. Each floor held a pair of suites plus a single. The bathroom was unisex. I roomed with two of my freshman-year roommates, Anselm (econ) and Sang (biology). Anna, Prudence, and Eunice lived in the mirroring suite. Bethany, a junior, had the coveted single.

My Bethany Blanket knowledge was scant. I knew she woke to the hopped-up strains of "Two Princes" at six-thirty every morning to jog in East Rock. She had an Anglo surname, but I sensed nuance about the eyes. She dressed like an expensive hippie or in clothes that made her look like a boy. I'd seen her lounging on Cross Campus with her California friends, whose rad intonations constituted a foreign language. She often wore a T-shirt that said "Milk" on the front and "It Does a Body Good" on the back. Later I learned her dad was lead attorney for the U.S. Dairy Farmers or something.

The first real time we said more than hi was a brisk Friday in October. Earlier I had gone to the dining hall with Massimo. The son of an Italian diplomat and a Mexican pistachio heiress, he was born in Cairo, spoke with a faint German accent, and had attended prep school near D.C., where he'd led a barbershop quartet and played lacrosse.

To his parents' dismay, Massimo wanted to be a writer. He was revising a story for his advanced fiction seminar, which he brought to dinner. He was going to work on it in the Saybrook library afterward. He had written "Untitled" at the top.

"You've got to put *something* there," I advised cheerfully.

"That's the title," he sniffed. " 'Untitled' is the title."

The seminar was taught by Trevor Stoops, author of *Trapezoids*. Some classes, Stoops would show up an hour late, then dazzle everyone with insights about their work. Students would repair to a nearby diner after, where he'd regale them with literary gossip. Other times, he appeared nervous and sad, once breaking down in tears and moaning, "Martha, Martha." He made up for it next class, bringing homemade cupcakes with the students' names frosted in red.

"Can I take a look?"

"Is not ready."

"I'm just curious."

"It's a work in progress."

I handed him my Walkman. "Listen while I read."

For the past few weeks, I'd been playing *Nevermind* nonstop, trying to decide if I liked it. I took the cassette box out and Massimo snorted at the cover: a naked baby in a pool, grabbing for a dollar bill on a fishhook.

"Is this a joke?"

I didn't think so. As far as I could tell, Nirvana had no trace of irony or playfulness, usually a sign of bad art, though sometimes the opposite. With a superior air, Massimo slipped on the headphones and pressed Play, while I read "Untitled." The story was about a day in the life of a teenager, "M." It was told in the third person, but I could easily spot the hero's resemblance to Massimo: he was also a baritone who played midfield. The writing was flat, and the dialogue sounded off, but at least I understood what was going on. After four pages, though, it shifted register so abruptly that I thought a page from a different story had been stapled in by mistake. It turned out that everything I'd just read was taking place on a giant "scan-screen" aboard a UFO shaped like the moon. Aliens were watching life on Earth unfold, bored out of their "cog-sacs," which was short for "cognition-sacs."

"Huh," I said. I flipped back to the first page, looking for clues.

Meanwhile, Massimo pursed his lips in distress. Thirty seconds into "Lithium," he looked decidedly unwell—eyes bulging, skin gray—and by song's end he was a gibbering wreck.

"No, no, no," he said. The headphones came off and he staggered away, cog-sac ruined.

I got a second dessert and steeped some tea, then sorted through the table tents. These were colored Xeroxes, folded across the middle so they could stand up. As the weekend approached, the tents multiplied with the wealth of diversions. The Yale Film Society was showing the director's cut of *Brazil*. The Alley Cats, an a cappella troupe, would be having a singing "jam" over in Davenport. There were auditions for *Measure for Measure* and a study break sponsored by Campus Crusade for Christ. A student improv troupe, Just Add Water, was performing at the Calhoun dining hall at nine. I had gone to a show once. They asked the audience for a vegetable, a president, and the title of a book, then crafted a skit on the fly. It was hilarious for the first two minutes. Then it made you hate the world.

That evening there was a double bill of Tom Stoppard one-acts, a night of traditional Indian dance, a lecture about the meat industry by a Scottish ethicist. Nothing appealed. Frankly, I was envious of my classmates' creative and organizational abilities. I had entered Yale aspiring to be an architect or a journalist, but who was I fooling? I was a history major, planning to apply to law school down the road. I vowed to do a lot of pro bono work, make peace with my soul.

On the message board by our door, Sang had scrawled an invitation to a rolling pickup game at Payne Whitney. I was no great shakes at hoops, but it seemed a solid last resort. The game started at seven and went on forever. I could drop in anytime. Presumably, our roommate Anselm would be with him.

I have to add this one thing. Back in the spring, on the day before they kicked us out of the dorms, a group of us tipsy malingerers had convened in one of the Wright Hall common rooms on the first floor of Wright Hall. Sang had already gone to Boston for an internship at a biotech firm, leaving Prudence, Massimo, his funny roommate Corwin, a track star named McVick, a violinist named Pearl, Anselm, and me. Everyone was loopy, after having survived our first year. People drifted in and out that night, displaying hidden talents. McVick picked up a guitar. Pearl did magic. I'm not good at describing clothes, but she wore vintage stuff as she performed a coin trick on a steamer trunk, passing her hands over a quarter, dime, nickel, penny, keeping up a stream of old-timey patter. The money vanished and reappeared in mind-boggling combinations, until at the end the change was all piled neatly in the center, in order of circumference.

"Damn," I said. "What's the trick called?"

"Oh, I don't know."

"Come on," Prudence said.

"You have to understand the context of the time."

"Tell us!" Massimo boomed.

At last she said, in a faint voice: "Chink-a-chink."

The name was so crazy it made us crazy. We gasped and cackled, rolled on the rug, slapped ourselves on the cheeks. I saw Pearl and Massimo wrapping their arms around each other.

"Chink-a-chink!" Corwin shrieked into my face, tears streaming. "What the hell!"

I somehow punched a hole in the side of the steamer trunk. It seemed the right thing to do. Eventually we all stopped heaving and hooting. We emptied the bottles. Anselm confessed to a weird dream in which our roommate, Sang, sat on his lap and played with his blond tresses. That was all he remembered. Anselm asked if I thought he had an Asian fetish; Sang—Korean like me—used that term when he saw a white guy going out with an Asian girl. I said it depended if he dreamt it more than once.

≈

But back to meeting Bethany. Dinner had made me sluggish. Before b-ball at the gym, I planned to shower, get through more of *The Gothic Image*. It was a book for my medieval history class, about religious art in France. I was a hundred pages behind. The previous owner had highlighted a single sentence in the introduction ("Work of the thirteenth century interests us even when inadequately executed for we feel there is something in it akin to a soul") before giving up. So far, I understood that one line perfectly, but not much else.

The third-floor bathroom had two showers, though when one was on, the other was reduced to a dribble. I entered the first stall with my shampoo caddy. The water came out full blast, but I stepped aside like a blasé ninja before the cold spray hit. That's when I saw the camcorder on the wall between the showers, secured by tons of masking tape.

The camera looked to be off and, in any case, was aimed down into the other stall. I entertained dark thoughts about Sang, who'd actually gone AWOL from his aforementioned internship, spending that precious summer in Boston taking pictures of street performers and old tombstones. Was he an innocent shutterbug or a Peeping Tom? How well did I really know him? He was pretty religious—his uncle was a pastor in New Jersey—but you never could tell.

I stepped out, threw on my robe, and opened the other curtain. Bethany Blanket was asleep on the tiled floor, in a blue bathing suit and white swim cap, a pair of goggles perched on her head. Her stall was bone-dry. She held a penlike object, attached to the camera by a black cord. She opened her eyes.

"Hello, Sang," she said.

"I'm not Sang."

"Are you sure?"

"Not all Asians look alike."

"That's true, but *you* two do." She sat up. "I'm half, myself."

"What are the halves?"

"My mother's from Hong Kong, and Dad's, like, ninety percent Dutch, ten percent we don't know."

I helped her up. Her fingers were cool and thin. The top of my robe slipped open as I pulled. I worried the belt would give. She picked a black thread off the shoulder and dropped it carefully in the trash, like a mama bird bringing a worm to the nest.

"Why were you on the floor?"

"Waiting for the sun to come through." Bethany went over to the window. Above the standard-issue panes was a half-circle of stained glass, like a mound of sherbet, showing a scholar or maybe a dragon. "When the light hits at a certain angle, the colors stream right into the shower. Noticed it a week ago. It was like swimming in a rainbow." She peeled off a three-inch strip of tape from the sticky mass stabilizing the camera. "I wanted to turn the shower on, then right as the water came out, I'd trigger the camera with this clicker."

Her recorder looked too small to capture such a sublime sight. "What happened?"

"I conked out." She yawned. "I pulled an all-nighter yesterday."

"I went to bed at three," I said in sympathy. "I had a Dada and Surrealism paper."

"I *thought* I saw you in that class."

My paper was on René Magritte. Lately I'd been captivated by any work of art that contained a work of art within it. A play within a play, a book within a book, a painting that depicted another, smaller painting. I had never paid attention to such things before. Was the interior work of art less "real" than the surrounding work? If so, why does our mind attribute levels of reality to what is, after all, just color on canvas? Since a painter can paint a painter painting a painting, could we ourselves be paintings, painted by some larger, divine painter—i.e., God? Pondering such things probably wouldn't help me get into law school, but I couldn't stop.

"I saw something like that at the Rep two weeks ago," Bethany said, attacking the tape clump again. This was the first time I'd seen a woman with unshaved armpits. The hairs were cute, like soft tufted animal ears. "A playwright writes a play in which a playwright writes a play."

"That's the spirit."

I'd finished a draft Wednesday, but late Thursday night I asked Anselm if it was too academic. ("We're literally *in the academy*," he said.) The painting in question, *La condition humaine,* depicted an easel in front of a window, the landscape on the canvas seamlessly merging with the "real" landscape we viewers assume is behind it—beyond the glass, "out there." How to convey its profound unease?

I gave Bethany the blow-by-blow: Just after midnight, I decided to interrogate the artwork's reality by framing my original paper as a mere *translation* of an essay by a fictional Belgian critic. I wrote a brief "preface" under my own name, then credited the rest to one Monsieur Hans de Krap. Were these my *real* thoughts on the subject if they were spouted by an invented writer? The idea of unstable reality would be reflected in the form of the piece.

"Whoa," she said. "I love that meta shit." She unpeeled a strip of tape and stuck it on my shoulder.

"I'm worried my TA won't get it." There were only two papers for the class, and I couldn't afford a low grade.

"The concept is what's important."

My TA, Win, had been a New York scenester before heading to graduate school. He let it slip, early in the term, that he'd once been a staple at Warhol's Factory, doing silkscreens and "people watching." Win was a tweedy, debate-team-looking guy who wore pinstripes and round tortoiseshell glasses, but this biographical information suggested hidden depths.

"What did you write about?" I asked Bethany.

"*Un chien andalou.*"

In the first class, Professor Burton showed us Dalí and Buñuel's film, a collaborative dream from 1928. When the man on the screen ran a razor across a woman's eye, a girl dashed out of the lecture hall, hand over her mouth. Nowadays, a teacher might give a trigger warning, but Professor Burton grasped the pedagogical value of shock. The day no one fled in disgust would be the day she retired.

"I thought it would be cool to run *Un chien* backward, see if it made more sense," Bethany said.

"Like listening for Satanic messages in 'Stairway to Heaven.' "

"The scene where they split her eye open now comes at the end, so it's like putting the eye back together. That was rad. Are you an art history major?"

"Just regular history," I said. "History without the art."

Bethany swore. She'd broken a nail trying to liberate the camera from its perch. "Here—lift me up."

"How did you even get it up there?" I asked.

"That tall chick Anna helped."

I held Bethany by the waist. She had the skeleton of a bird, but I could barely move her.

"Not like that," she said. I felt her breath on my face. "Put me on your shoulders."

Damp legs clamped my neck. I got up from my crouch slowly, not wanting to slip. My head had a limited range of motion. I stared at the tiles and the drain, her thigh-flesh warming my cheeks. We were like a mythological creature, designed to play a specific role in an undergraduate allegory. Bethany whistled "Two Princes" as she clawed at the tape. With a satisfying rip, the major strips came free.

"Down, boy," she said.

I crouched to let her slip off my shoulders and we left the stall. Bethany studied the camera's flip-out screen to see if anything had been recorded. Nada. She ejected the small cassette, frowned, put it back in. We exited the bathroom at last. There was a rambling note on the Yale Crew bulletin board tacked to her door. I could only make out the word *Sorry!*

"Everything all right?"

"Today's your lucky day, Joon."

"My name is Ed." She must have seen last year's photo directory, which mixed up my middle name with my first. My grandmother in Korea was the only one who called me Joon anymore.

"Your stage name should be Joon."

"Huh?"

"You're going to be in my movie."

"I'm not an actor."

"You're acting right now."

"I don't think so."

"We're all actors, from the moment we wake up in the morning."

"Not me."

"Put on some clothes and let's get cracking. A solid top, just not black or white."

"Excuse me?"

"You've passed the audition."

≈

My alternatives were basketball or closing the gap with *The Gothic Image,* so I changed into a sweater and jeans and busted out the J.Crew barn jacket my mom had sent me. When I came out, Bethany was in a yellow tracksuit, a fuzzy hand-loomed bag slung across her shoulder. We left Saybrook behind. The air was turning crisp and the days were getting short.

"How much am I getting for this?"

"I'll treat you to Claire's."

Claire's Corner Copia was a vegetarian place I disliked because it reminded me of Yuna Cho, my hostile ex-girlfriend. She was the first vegetarian I had met in my life, let alone Korean vegetarian, and the novelty had apparently been irresistible. We had gone out a couple months freshman year, but her parents pressured her to break up. Something to do with the province my parents hailed from in Korea. I imagined our ancestors living in rival villages, stoking a centuries-old blood feud. It didn't faze me at first. Then over the summer I sent her an insane twenty-page letter explaining why we were meant to be together, with a few paragraphs of NC-17 content. Yuna replied with a Buddhist parable about filial piety in which a daughter cut flesh from her leg to feed her starving father. That seemed like overkill. Now, when I saw her on campus, I made tracks the other way.

Naturally, as soon as we got to Claire's, I spotted Yuna in a corner booth, holding court with three other officers of KASY, which stood for Korean American Students at Yale. She had some standing in the group, and seemed to be prepping for a coup. I kept my head down. Bethany Blanket ordered a salad for herself and coffee for me. She looked more Asian in the murky lighting, the Dutch side relinquishing control.

"You'd better have some coffee," she said, checking her watch. The waitress came by with a huge pale dinner roll. "We'll be shooting all night."

I was getting cold feet. Had I lost my mind?

"Don't worry, there's no nudity."

"Your loss."

She snickered. "So what's the problem?"

"I don't like hearing myself on tape," I explained. "Seeing myself on camera will be worse."

"No one's forcing you to watch. You can do it and never think of it again."

I hadn't thought of it that way. Bethany lit up a cigarette. You could still smoke in most restaurants then, though I'm not sure you could at Claire's. I looked across the room at Yuna Cho, who was staring at me. I turned to study the menu on the wall.

"Do you know her?" Bethany asked.

"Who?"

"Crazy-looking chick."

"No comment."

"In the Benetton sweater."

"Never seen her."

"She looks familiar. Is she in Saybrook?"

"Trumbull—oh."

"Busted. Stay right here."

Yuna's friends had dispersed. They were waiting outside under a cone of light at the corner of Chapel Street, while Yuna added a few more coins to the tip. She was fastidious about using up change. Already I could see what was going to happen. I thought about how the Surrealists switched theaters halfway through a movie, so they could catch part of another feature, the start of a newsreel, a few gags in a comic short, then mentally stitch the bits together into one exquisite thing. The coherence of incoherence. I wanted to skip over to another story, but I was trapped in this one, the one in which Bethany Blanket summoned Yuna Cho to our table and asked disingenuously if she'd acted before.

"Not since high school," Yuna said. "I was Major-General Stanley in *Pirates of Penzance*."

"That's a dude."

"It was an all-girls school."

"*Right*." Bethany tore apart her dinner roll and gave me half. "Do you know Joon?"

"I'm Yuna," she said. "Hello, Joon."

My head felt light. What was going on? Yuna's playful side was coming out. I couldn't remember whether I liked that or not.

"Hi," I said, continuing the charade. We shook hands.

"Joon's majoring in Dada and Surrealism. How about you?"

"Chemistry."

"Good choice," Bethany said. "You can do anything you want with that degree."

That's when I noticed the camera welded to her face. "You're filming this?"

"Keep going! Don't mind me!"

"It's just a screen test," Yuna said. "Right?"

"Mm-hmm. Act natural, Joon. Not so uptight. Act like you would if you were just meeting a pretty girl."

"I would act uptight," I said, "*if* she were pretty."

"Come on, dude. She's a knockout."

Yuna tilted her head coquettishly. She looked the same but different. She was wearing earrings, a chunky necklace I hadn't seen before.

"Don't flatter yourself," I grumbled. To Bethany I said, "What's the movie about?"

"Don't talk to *me*, talk to *Yuna*."

"I have nothing to say to her."

"Good. Use the aggression." She didn't know about the breakup, the anguish, the intergenerational provincial prejudice. She wiggled her fingers in a *More, more* gesture.

"Excuse me," the waitress said to Bethany. "You're not allowed to film here."

"I have a permit."

"Restaurant policy."

Bethany smoothly trained the camera on the waitress, who happened to be Eunice, the comp lit major from Entryway D. A volume of Camus was in her apron.

"Seriously, I'm going to call security."

"Seriously, I'm going to call security," Bethany mimicked.

"Also, no smoking."

Outside, Yuna's KASY friends looked at me askance. I recognized Jay and Michelle but not the third person. Jay was a senior who'd had designs on Yuna last year, when we were going out. She had told Jay that he looked too much like her brother for her to feel any attraction. Short of plastic surgery, there was nothing he could do. He was a buff fencer, and I think he wanted to kill me.

They'd all left by the time Bethany paid the bill.

"My life goal," our director said, leading us back toward campus, "is to make twelve full-length features—then stop."

"You don't want to wear out your welcome," Yuna joked.

"It's not that. I like the idea of someone watching all my films, back to back. A true devotee. If each one is two hours long, then that's one full day out of that person's life. A Bethany Blanket retrospective."

"What's your favorite movie?" I asked.

"I don't want you to have any preconceptions." She lit a new cigarette. "My pet peeve is when I see an actor in one movie, playing a pirate, say, and then in the next one he's a doctor or farmer."

"That's called range," Yuna said.

"Sure," Bethany said, hustling to my right. The camera was back in her hand. I hadn't noticed we were "rolling."

"But in my head, I can never totally forget the earlier roles," she continued. "I can only fall in love with a movie when I know nothing beforehand. A totally fresh experience."

"So in your perfect world," I said, "an actor does a single movie and then retires?"

"They don't have to retire. I just don't want to see anything else they're in."

We stopped for the light. Three big leaves blew past us on the crosswalk, moving end over end like a dance troupe hurling itself into a big finale. When we could go, Bethany faced us and walked backward, shooting. "Make sure I don't trip!"

"Does this movie count as one of the twelve?" Yuna asked.

"Probably not!"

Yuna looked sore, like maybe she'd bail even before it began. "Promise us this will be one of the twelve."

"I can't!"

"Bitch."

Bethany made the *More, more* gesture. She was pushing our buttons. We were passing Payne Whitney, monstrously tall in the dark. I thought of Anselm and Sang and the basketball game inside. I could ditch Bethany and Yuna, abandon this impromptu shoot.

"Where are we headed?" I asked.

"Machine City."

"Eww." Yuna wrinkled her nose. I had to admit, she was cute. "Why?"

"That's the title of the movie."

Machine City was the nickname of the gloomy lounge under Cross Campus Library. The library itself, plunged belowground, was morose to begin with: clinically lit and drably carpeted, ringed by a series of grim concentration closets known as weenie bins. But Machine City was the next layer of hell. You never went there willingly. It looked like a holdover from a '70s dystopian flick, the bunker where humanity's last survivors huddle before melting into radioactive goop.

Chain-smokers kept the air warm and terrible. Particularly sadistic TAs held office hours here. Students crammed for exams at Formica tables under flyspecked lamps, ringed by the vending machines that gave the place its name. Littering the glass fronts were outraged notes from those who'd slid in bills and received neither change nor sustenance. The water fountain never worked, and the microwave made a strange noise if you entered a time over fifty-nine seconds. The name of the space was ironic: this was where technology came to die.

"I can't do this without a script," Yuna said, somehow even more luminous under the crap fluorescents.

Bethany gave her a single piece of paper with the title printed at the top. She replaced the tape, put in another, capturing it all. I'd never seen videocassettes this small—half the size of my Nirvana tape. She could shoot all night.

"This just says, 'The artist makes love to the robot,'" Yuna griped.

"It's a prompt."

"Which one am I?" Yuna asked. "The artist or the robot?"

Bethany gave me a look, my cue to explain.

"That's the question, isn't it?" I said, and proceeded to give a brief history of Dadaism. Professor Burton's lectures had left a big impression on me, and I proved a faithful parrot. "Basically, the sex drive is reduced to a mechanical process, as seen in, uh, all those paintings of coffee grinders."

"I have no clue what you're saying, as always."

"It's a starting point," Bethany said optimistically.

Yuna considered the premise some more.

"Okay," she said. "Let's do this."

≈

We stayed in Machine City till closing. Bethany changed her mini-tapes two more times. At one point she paused to pull props from her bag. She gave me a wig and made up my face to look old, while Yuna slipped into a lavender sweatsuit Bethany had brought. Yuna was the robot, ageless, and I was the decrepit artist.

Bethany gave minimal direction. She let us talk. Half the banter had some basis in reality; the rest we made up. Yuna conjured a decent crying scene at a key moment.

Toward the end, Bethany gave her a pair of sunglasses. "Now say something true."

After a dramatic pause, Yuna said, "I'm seeing someone. Someone you know."

"Okay," I said. Yuna had a sad, superior air. She wanted me to think. To name her partner. "I give up."

"You see him every day."

"Sang?"

She mimed barfing.

"Ken Griffey Jr.?" A poster of the ballplayer hung by his bed.

"What? No. It's Anselm."

"*My* Anselm?"

"We have a lot in common."

"Sure you do. You must be out of your mind."

"Don't be a jerk."

"Anselm has an Asian fetish."

"That doesn't exist," she said confidently. "There's no such thing."

"Oh, Anselm," I sighed. "I should have known."

"He's meeting my parents next weekend."

"Wonderful. I'm sure they'll be thrilled his family isn't from the wrong province or whatever. They aren't even from the same continent. Just perfect. Very happy for you."

"Anselm thought you'd be cool with it. I told him not to say anything. I knew you'd be a fucking maniac."

I turned to the camera. "Am I being a maniac?"

Bethany Blanket said, "And . . . cut!"

That night, when I was alone in bed, my mind raced. I had acted in a movie. I had said too much. Was the character a sympathetic one? Well developed? We had talked a lot, Yuna and I, more than we had since the semester began. Now there was this Anselm situation. I wondered how Sang would take it. Life was complicated. I thought of Massimo hearing Nirvana for the first time, and of his untitled story, which I still had in my backpack. I thought of René Magritte in Brussels, wearing a bowler hat, putting the finishing touches on *La condition humaine.* I thought of Dalí and Buñuel, procuring a calf's eye to cut with a razor. How did they get it, who pried it out? I thought of the lyrics to "Lithium," or really just the part where Kurt Cobain sings, "I'm not going to crack."

≈

All of this is ancient history. Yuna and Anselm stayed together through graduation, then moved to Minnesota, where the trail goes cold. Sang I've kept in touch with. We grab a drink once in a while, talk sports and kids and home renovation projects.

After *Machine City* ended its weekend run, Bethany and I barely saw each other. Later someone told me she had a new boyfriend who was a mason in Hamden—not a secret-society Freemason, but a guy who worked with bricks. She spent spring term in Rome, moved off campus senior year with some crew buds. I ran into her just once, outside of Atticus Books. She said something about making another movie, but it wasn't an invitation.

In truth, I hadn't thought of Bethany Blanket in twenty-odd years, until I saw my reflection in the elevator this morning. Now I've spent a solid day wading through memories, scouring the internet. The alumni site says they tore down Machine City over a decade ago. I had no idea. The one photo I can find doesn't look real, more like a picture of a picture.

It's late where I am. Everyone left work hours ago. The rain has stopped, and I'm alone in the office with my expensive view of the shipless river. Even the sailors have gone home. A week ago, I put in a bid on the sweater Kurt Cobain wore on *MTV Unplugged,* and there's thirteen minutes till the online auction ends. I just upped my max bid. They let you set your ceiling till the last minute. Then you're locked in.

This laptop's so hot it might burn my leg. In all my years at the firm, I've never done pro bono. From what I can tell, Bethany Blanket moved back to L.A. after graduation, where she worked on some movies you've heard of, others that went straight to video. She never made a feature, let alone a dozen. IMDb claims she popped up in early-aughts cop shows, as a pretty corpse or a distraught friend. Google tells me she has a degree in social work. LinkedIn says her last job was three years ago, marketing for a jewelry company. We all end up doing something.

I'm going to try to raise the ceiling one last time.

AN ACCURATE ACCOUNT

February 14, 2014
My dearest nephew,

I assure you this late reply is a function of my current status—stranded in Tokyo with a dozen uncomprehending actors—not to mention the scale of your ask. You wanted to know what it was like for me starting out, armed (as you soon will be) with just a BA in communications from Penumbra College. Who was I, before my first play, prior to my fame as the pioneer of the postmodern twist ending, when I didn't yet know my path? I.e., who was I when I was more or less like you? Confucius say: Short letter, tall order. In your postscript you mention wanting to be a playwright like your semi-senile uncle, and that anything I could say would be of enormous help. So here it goes, my nephew. Here it goes.

All of this happened back in the '90s, *up* in the 90s: 1992, East 92d Street, off First. I was living in the basement of a townhouse owned by my older and better-looking cousin, Tom. He and his wife, Archy, ran the transcription business on the ground floor, where I worked a few nights a week, typing out the dialogue from a public access show. These were usually byzantine community squabbles, lensed for maximum glare, hosted by a forceful woman with coppery lips, coppery hair. I would have to type "[*shouting*]" in brackets so much that I made it one of my paste commands. The show often featured a squinting codger who expounded on money and the Masons, the cryptic intricacies of the one-dollar bill.

All of it was strangely comforting. As crazy as I felt back then, I knew I still had a ways to go before I lost my mind completely.

Even at 22, I wanted to write for the stage, but for the time being, I typed for the hearing-impaired. The characters were not of my choosing. The home row of the word processor tended to stick, so that sometimes I'd be tapping along and realize too late that the text was a paragraph behind the voices. I would have to rewind the VCR, which also liked to jam, meaning a small eternity might be lost searching for the spot where things went off the rails.

My cousin Tom would swoop in at random and tell me to hit Print. Then he'd sit with the script before him, lassoing errors with a red pen. "Quinn," he'd say, "we want an accurate account. Nothing more, nothing less." Tom had been like a favorite uncle when I was a kid, but now those four words were almost all he cared to say to me. His hospitality extended only to the low rent. I made it my mission to move in a year.

The night shift fell to me twice a week. During the day, a trio of freelancers would occupy the space. Archy, his wife, was supposed to be transcribing as well, but she had a weakness for three-hour lunch breaks at Bloomie's. Her work always trailed off, incomplete. Most evenings I'd come to my desk to find a pulsing cursor and a Post-it pleading, "Quinn—Could you clean this up for me? XO Archy." Sometimes she'd leave a Medium Brown Bag with undershirts and boxers, just my size.

It soon fell to me to finish her transcripts and ensure that *her* account was accurate. I figured it was the price of staying at their place on East 92nd before I found my feet, and started my real life.

Tom and Archy lived on the second and third floors. Archy was French, or had spent time in France, and would correct me, saying their rooms were on the "first and second" floors. In Paris, you see, the ground floor—the office—would be equivalent to zero. It didn't really matter to me. The basement, where I lived, was still the basement. Or perhaps it was negative one.

They didn't have kids, but had been trying for a while. I knew this because even though I was secreted in the cellar, through an acoustical fluke I could hear everything that happened on the third or second floor. Mostly it was a symphony of the mundane: the radio's drone and the dishwasher's chug, the clothes dryer's arrhythmia and the microwave's triple beep. I was occasionally privy to the more secret sounds of frantic coupling, the banging of a headboard I'd never seen but imagined to have a Wild West theme, rustic timber rustled up from a distressed Nebraska dude ranch.

Either my cousin or his wife wept in the shower every morning, low sobs that filtered through the plumbing to hit me belowdecks with startling clarity. Maybe they both wept, on alternating days. As I get older, I think that's what it was. Crying was the price *they* paid, for the beautiful townhouse, the weekend antiquing, the view of the river to the east.

Late at night I'd drift off to the sound of their TV, toggling between news and reruns. Silence meant a fight. She'd turn off *Cheers* and say, "New York is full of unreliable people and I hate them." Or she'd hit Mute on *Mad About You* and declare, "Stupid people should be executed, including the guy at the deli." If Tom began to respond, she'd say, "Let me finish," the volume rising sharply across that short sentence.

It seemed that every syllable was a step along the trail to the fertility clinic on the other side of the park. They would discuss upcoming appointments, then how the appointments went, then the results from the appointments. They talked about how much money they were spending. When they were optimistic they thought of names. Nico or Hunter if it was a boy, Maya or Devon for a girl.

"What about Quinn?" Archy asked one night.

"What about him?" Tom said. "If my cousin's bugging you, say the word. We can use the basement for storage."

"No," said Archy. "For a name."

Tom laughed. "Quinn's a little queer."

Me in brackets: [*raises eyebrows*].

"I'm adding it to the list," she said.

Winter came and the basement was cold, the window glazed with ice. I bought a space heater that made a purring sound but did not actually produce heat. It was like the idea of a cat. Archy left a bag of gently worn pashminas, which I positioned around my shoulders. I looked like FDR at Yalta.

In January, the attic tenant died. Maybe *he'd* been the shower sobber. We called him Oslo because he came from Norway in the early '60s, though he never quite found his way around the language. He'd lived in the house long before Tom bought it. Archy and I hauled out three decades of cigar boxes and indecipherable stag magazines, as the cold made dragons of us, our breath taking form in the tentlike room.

My very tentative Valentine's date with the hottie where I barbacked fell through, so I spent the night scanning the ads of *The Village Voice*. I needed a new place, a better job, probably furniture as well.

To fall asleep I read the smut salvaged from the stash of my erstwhile housemate. I say I read the smut because that's what it was, imageless erotic accounts composed in Norwegian. I could make out every fifth or fiftieth word. Many were wild guesses. It left a lot to the imagination, but I found it enriching.

As I brushed my teeth I heard Tom say: "We could adopt. I think we need to think about adoption, Archy."

"And then what happens if we get pregnant right after?" she said.

"What are you talking about?"

"Let me finish. I know people this has happened to. They adopt one and then get knocked up naturally. Then we have two right out of the gate. We might as well adopt triplets. Why don't we adopt triplets, Tom?"

"Archy, you're not making sense. I'm just looking at reality."

"Let's do something now," she said.

"Archy, we're not at our best. Why don't we call it a day."

"Try one more time for me."

"I'm not 100% in the mood, to be perfectly honest."

"Try anyway," she said.

"There's a limit to trying," he said after a while.

Then I heard something break.

My dearest nephew, I can recall this scene because I started transcribing as the argument swelled. It was the seed from which my first play, *Emergency on West 92nd,* grew. The raw dialogue is in front of me as I write this letter. But what I never put down, until this moment, is what happened after the row. How Archy slipped into the basement, catching me by surprise with the Scandinavian word-porn in hand, with my Norwegian wood, as it were.

In brackets: "[*Puts down magazine*]."

"Hey, Archy," I said, as though her presence in my room at midnight were routine. "I was just getting ready to—"

She put a finger to my lips and whispered: "Let me finish, Quinn."

Two weeks later I moved to a sublet on Beekman Place, and a year after that to East 6th, then to Carroll Gardens for fifteen years; now Tokyo, where my life is unreal.

Perhaps you've already figured out that this is a story about your parents. That Tom's name is Ted, and Archy's Abby, and Ted was not my cousin, but my brother, may he rest in peace.

I wish I could come back for commencement. Penumbra is lovely in the spring. I wish I were in New York to help you settle in, find inspiration. But maybe, Quinn, this "accurate account" of why your name is the same as mine will be enough to get you started. . . . Your loving uncle, DAD.

THE AIR AS AIR

DAD'S A HARD nut to crack; in fact, he's all nut, or all shell, through and through. Solid, is what I'm saying. Impossible. Makes me call him the Big Man, even though I'm taller. Doesn't listen, not at all. The ears are pure show. I mean, I love him, but there's a limit.

Take this one time last spring. He was in town, not exactly my town, but West Eucalyptus. Call it forty miles south by crow, a hundred if we're talking roadway reality. Add an hour or three if you're like me and tend to get lost. It is on the water. He was there alone, no wife. Could I come up? He meant down. I borrowed Cyn's car and made the drive through sheets of rain. A deep-tissue massage for the Honda. I drove slowly and had plenty of time to practice my breathing. It was a challenge. Individuated nostriling. Silently-deeply, silently-deeply. You want to feel the wind caress each nasal hair.

My breathing is the most important thing to me these days, thanks to Karl Ababa and his teachings. Folks think the war's why I'm all Ababa, all the time. I got knocked around toward the end, it's true. My leg now is not my leg then. There are things in my head that are never coming out. Something bad happened to my lips as well. Taken as a totality, I couldn't advise enlistment. But the hurt that needs to heal goes deeper than that, back to what Ababa calls the First Bad Breath. It's the same way for everybody.

Master Ababa speaks of the lungs as wings we keep folded, unaware that we can fly. He writes of the mystery he calls the Cough That Disappears. We have to recognize not just the act of breathing but the history of breathing. He says that in pursuit of the Higher Ventilation we should take Faint Breaths and "ask the unanswerable of ourselves." Maybe so. But I don't think he means questions like *Why was the Big Man in West Eucalyptus?*

My father lives all the way in Taiwan now, where he chairs the welding department at Fuxing Normal University. Taiwan seems random for a white guy named Cal Felix from Peekskill, New York, but a plush gig is a plush gig. He has a driver, a Beemer, a Taoist dietitian. He has a brutalist townhouse, infinity pool on the roof.

It had been a year-plus since the Big Man and I last saw each other, and we hadn't spoken since. This was all my fault somehow. He knew about the breathing regimen, and I could feel him raising his eyebrows at me from an ocean away. In his mind I'd signed up with some cult. Karl Ababa would say my dad was "breathing with the wrong lung."

The old me would say that half the reason I enlisted was because the Big Man had been in the service, but I am giving myself permission to own my wounds from here on out.

Ashley—that's his wife—is actually pretty sympathetic to what I'm getting at. She's been with the Big Man for five years now. Third wife, very short. Her job involves holograms that live inside your phone. The Big Man met her at a noodle shop during the rainy season. There's some cute story that goes here, but I think I've repressed it.

The storm had rolled out to sea by the time I hit West Eucalyptus, and I drove the last few miles with the windows down. I had been afraid of the water, but now the air was clear, circulating through the car like the car was a lung. A boat-shaped cloud chased a cloud-shaped cloud, and my eyes followed them until a mountain got in the way.

The breeze freed fat drops from the trees as I walked from the parking lot to the turquoise motel. Around the corner, a worker was standing by a ladder while his partner, unseen, narrated something in Spanish from the roof. Little green lizards and red crabs bright as poker chips scurried from my path. I'd never seen that before—small red crabs walking around on people turf—and I got a little upwelling of wonder right in my heart. I imagined going through life sidewise. What was I talking about? I already *was* doing that. I looked to the water and did a little silently-deeply. No boats were out, and the ocean looked tight as cellophane.

The Big Man was waiting in the lobby, reading a paper. It was just the local rag, the *Eucalyptus Bee,* but he was reading as though it had the scoop on secret financial shudderings that would affect his portfolio if he didn't act decisively. His hands were in fists. His face was like a fist. His legs flexed angrily, somehow also fistlike, under cargo shorts emblazoned with Fuxing Normal's insignia, which looks like a city rising from the waves. Or sinking. Or maybe it's just some buildings by the water. His strong chest filled out a faded black polo shirt. He looked more or less like his Gmail portrait. More hair had evaporated from his head; really, it prospered only around his ears. His eyebrows, meanwhile, had gained ground. In some ways he looked about a million years old, but his overall intensity gave him vigor. Negative vigor but vigor nonetheless.

Part of me wanted to walk backward quietly to the car, clocking the alveoli, silently-deeply, and drive the hundred miles home. Home to Cyn and serious breathing, home to marathon meditations on the teachings of Karl Ababa. I had forgotten to bring his latest book with me, *The Eyes Are Lungs*. It was six hundred pages long, another masterpiece. If I were home, Cyn and I could read passages to each other in bed—or, rather, I could read them and she could meditate on them and fall asleep.

Then the Big Man looked up and I was trapped. "I can't believe I'm missing this," he said, pointing at a wire story. A two-thousand-pound alligator had been captured off the western coast of Taiwan. It had taken thirty men to subdue it—not just thirty random men, but police, a pro wrestler, a full set of buff dudes. The alligator looked plastic in the picture, like parts of it were melting under the heat of a desk lamp. They were going to put it in a zoo.

He sighed. Sighing is the worst form of breathing and I try not to do it myself but I admit it's hard. Sighing is something we all struggle to unlearn.

In the margin was a doodle like a bar code. I could see how deep he'd made the lines. "Wonder why no one's called me. What do you think, Sidney—should I call? They have no idea what they're getting into. You need redundant caging. It's got to be stronger than strong." He added more lines to his sketch. "No one knows how to do that anymore," he said.

A familiar Big Man refrain. Things were better way back when. I tried to make of my mind a bottle of ink, pour it over his words. Mind is breath, I told myself, closing my eyes. But wait: you can't breathe ink. I was getting lost in abstraction, one of Ababa's Three Deadly Deals. In a second I was sputtering, choking.

"Hey, Mahatma Gandhi," he said. "Snap out of it."

"I'm doing my breathing."

"Sure, your breathing. Important to do the breathing. So many people forget to do the breathing nowadays." He cackled, his face up close. "You look tired, Sidney."

"This is how I always look." Did I lisp? I can't tell anymore. I watched a worker standing by the ladder outside. Every so often a rope end would get flung down from the roof and the man would tie it to a two-by-four or else just stare at it in disbelief: *Another rope?*

"You look like you've been eating chalk, son."

"I haven't been eating chalk."

"Can I buy you a rib eye?"

The Big Man was under the assumption that I was a vegetarian. I was, but I would fool him. "A steak would hit the spot," I said.

He chucked the newspaper and asked the desk lady where he could find the hotel restaurant.

She shook her head. "This is a motel."

He looked at me like all the failings of California, and possibly America, were wrapped up in that reply. We aimed ourselves at a place down the road with a fake windmill. The Big Man was in his usual rush. It was funny to see him walking so fast in the middle of nowhere. Funny and sad. There wasn't anyone watching except for some gulls. This wasn't Taipei, people flooding every intersection, masks over mouths.

"I saw all these beautiful red crabs on the pavement when I was walking to the hotel," I said.

"So you want crab? Maybe we can order crab."

"No, I mean there were these small crabs walking around, sidewise." I inhaled silently-deeply through my right nostril. Two clouds were merging overhead, stifling the sun.

"What are you doing in California?" I asked.

"I thought I told you on the phone."

"We didn't talk on the phone. You sent me an email."

"So."

"Yes?"

"So."

"Yes?"

"So you know about Uncle Buck," he said.

"The movie?"

"What movie? I'm talking about your Uncle Buck. He went on that show where they give you a makeover. It was Lindy's idea, the whole stupid TV thing. She had connections. You know Buck. He dresses worse than I do. He dresses like he smeared rubber cement on his chest and rolled around in a pile of old undershirts. So they shot the episode and it went a little too well, if you get my gist."

We were at the restaurant, more of a tavern situation. The neon sign in the window said BARBARA'S STEAKHOUSE, except BARBARA'S was burned out and so were the E and the A. It looked like ST KHOUSE, a hallowed name.

"So last week I get this text from Aunt Lindy saying Buck left her for one of the guys on the show. Can you believe it? The skinny one with the beard."

"I've never watched it."

The Big Man looked dubious. "Not the fat one with the goatee. The skinny one with the beard. Like a full beard."

"I don't know anything about anything."

"That is a fact." More cackling from the Big Man. We found a table in the back. "It's surprising above all else. That the skinny one would go for Uncle Buck. I don't know. The fat one, I could believe. But the skinny one! Buck is family and all, but he is not exactly fascinating. Not on any level. Have you ever had a fascinating conversation with him? I don't think it's possible. So that's why I'm here. He lives in Eucalyptus with the TV guy. Lindy wants me to talk some sense. But first I have to find him."

"Maybe he's in here," I said, looking around. It had been a decade, easy, since I'd last seen Uncle Buck. He could have been the bartender; I wouldn't have recognized him.

"Sit anywhere we want?" my father asked a waitress. She could have been Aunt Lindy, for all I knew.

"Sure."

"Can I leave my bag somewhere?"

"I'll put it up front."

"I don't like eating with a bag," he confessed to me, like a man of the world. "It's low-class. How's Cecilia?"

"You mean Cyn." I could hear myself say it like *thin*. "She's fine."

"Cindy, right. Did I meet her just that once, in Taipei? She loved that Buddha-head fruit."

"That's correct." I silently-deeply accepted air with my left nostril, exhaled half the bounty through my mouth, half through the right nostril.

"Ugliest produce I've ever seen, and that includes our friend the pomegranate. But I can't disagree with the flavor. Haven't had it in a long time. I've been eating guava and bananas mostly. Ashley's big on dragon fruit. She makes these smoothies. Nectar of the gods. Cindy make you smoothies?"

He apparently was not going to stop calling her Cindy. "No. We don't have a blender."

"Why not?"

"It doesn't seem essential. We're trying to pare down." This was in line with the teachings of Karl Ababa, though the master didn't really come out and say it. Mostly it was that money had been tight and we'd had to sell some things. A lot of things. We were basically down to two laptops and a toaster oven.

"I'm getting you a blender." He banged a fist on the table and smiled, like this was something I would remember. "A Taiwanese blender. Tatung, solid brand, you can throw it off a balcony and it still runs great. Ashley'll ship it to you, no problem." He thumbed out the order on his BlackBerry. I pictured Ashley in a vast storeroom, fulfilling my father's intercontinental whims. "Your girl is going to love it. You mean she's never had a smoothie in her life?"

"That's not what I said. I'm sure Cyn's had a smoothie. Everyone's had smoothies."

"Don't be so sure."

"I'm pretty certain."

"Where did she have one?"

"I don't know. Growing up. At parties. Everywhere. She might be sipping a smoothie as we speak."

"Has she had bubble tea?"

"Yes, we have bubble tea in California."

"It's a Taiwanese invention."

"I knew that," I lied.

The Big Man looked skeptical. "She still doing that band, the Supertramps?"

"Tramp Stamp," I said. "No, they broke up."

He nodded sagely and worked a finger into a thicketed ear. "Artistic differences."

"Sure."

"Like the Beatles."

"Kind of, yes." That was a stretch. What had really happened was that the bass player thought everyone should change their surnames to Tramp, and Cyn wasn't feeling it. Now she was studying, preparing to go back to school for ethnobotany. Our house was filled with flowers. It was beautiful but hell on the breathing.

From where I sat, I could see our motel. The workers were loading up their truck, which looked newly polished. They were done fixing whatever was broken, or else had just called it a day. No more rope ends hanging down. The ladder lay on its side near the door. It looked peaceful, at rest. It looked like it was conscious of its breathing.

Karl Ababa writes that everything in the world can be said to breathe. Not just people and animals. "The rocks and the trees breathe," he writes, "and the sidewalks and the pavings breathe, the water and the air itself all breathe." The air itself! It sounded completely nutty to me at first, but as I pass each level, I see the truth of his statements with greater clarity. The ladder was breathing, just as I was breathing. The restaurant was breathing, just as the motel was breathing, just as all the crabs and all the gulls were breathing.

The Big Man's voice plucked me out of my inhale-exhale zone. "How are they treating you down at Sempi?" he asked.

I had no idea what he meant. Then I remembered my old job. The one I'd ditched a year ago. Either the Big Man was in total denial or I'd never even told him.

It was unreal, that existence. After the army, I had landed at a Pasadena hedge fund called Sempiternal Analytix. It was as weird as the war. Psychopaths in office casual, USC pennants on the wall. All the guys talked fast, used nouns as verbs, verbs as nouns. Surface the spend. Table the thrash. They loved to hear themselves produce language. And there I was with my lips that didn't work.

"I'm taking a leave of absence," I told the Big Man, then confessed about two seconds later: "That's not true. I'm not at Sempi anymore and I'm never going back."

The waitress came, and we ordered. I was pretty sure she wasn't Aunt Lindy, unless Aunt Lindy now had a Mexican accent and was possibly still in high school.

"Not a bad idea, quit the rat race," the Big Man said. "And so."

"Yes?" I said a silent prayer to St. Khouse, heavenly protector of awkward dining companions.

"And so."

"Yes?"

"How are you?"

"Very fine, sir."

"You're feeling fine?"

"Just fine."

"Leg?"

"Beautiful."

On the walls were photos of actresses I didn't recognize, film stills and headshots from another era. An ingenue with a dagger, a brassy broad filing her nails, a woman from the future with a laser blaster. It took me a while to see that they were all the same actress.

"Your lips look good," the Big Man said.

"Thanks. Cyn does my makeup."

"Son. What is it you do these days? Besides the breathing."

Silently, deeply. Mostly besides the breathing I play video games, the ones that the Institute approves of. But three times a week I put on a uniform.

"I've got a pretty stable thing," I said, and knew right away that it wasn't. What had I been telling myself? "I'm at a Captain Clark's, one of the newer branches."

His eyebrows did about five different things. "It's, what, managerial?"

"Well, I do have to manage things," I said, meaning mostly manage my anger, my breathing, my brain.

Each day before my shift, a split second before I walk into the store, my old instincts come back. I hustle and hunch, scan for snipers. Very rarely, there are moments, seconds, when I imagine everyone dead. A loud noise and an arm here, a sneaker there. Bodies without heads and heads without eyes. A pair of lips kissing the floor forever. But mostly I am the picture of calm in my tropical shirt, holding a sign that says END OF LINE, so that customers know where to queue up. The lines can get seriously long, and for most of my shift there are two going at once. It can get stressful, but I like to think my peaceful manner settles a lot of nerves. Especially around five-thirty, the people hitting Captain Clark's right after work are stressed and ready to snap. My job is to sympathize, soothe. The sign isn't heavy for the first ten minutes. Then it might as well be made of stone.

"There are two lines, moving forward," I'd say. They told me to say it. It didn't make much sense, *moving forward*. But corporate linguists must have weighed the words, found their sequence of syllables relieving. *Two lines, moving forward*. It didn't hurt me any to say it. It meant that the lines weren't just stagnant. Even when they didn't appear to be moving, there was movement taking place. Shiftings at the molecular level.

Also I liked that I could say it without lisping. Maybe that's why they'd worded it the way they did. People can be very kind. If that's even true.

What made me quit Sempiternal Analytix? The interviewer in my head asks this. In my mind I cross my legs with ease and say: *The First and Deepest Breath*. Ababa's most famous book. Also his most important. Just because it's the most popular doesn't mean it's dumbed down. Everything you need is in there.

You probably saw it before I did. The famous cover with two clouds, blue and red, the edges overlapping in the middle. But I'd been away so long, out of the country, that there were things I didn't know. I found Master Karl's book in the seat-back pocket on my flight back home. My leg sang with titanium, and my mouth lay under Vaseline, but as my eyes moved over the words, certain sentences stuck. Here's one: "What if the story of your life, the one that you keep telling yourself, is not the right story?" He said to imagine a book in which the chapters could be read in any order, or skipped, erased, rewritten. Then to imagine the pages *made of air.*

The First and Deepest Breath came with me to my apartment off La Floridita, but it sat on the shelf while I got myself together. I had other things on my mind. Master Karl would say I was not ready to inhale what was already all around me. I was not seeing the air as air. I was not seeing it at all.

Then one night I saw an ad for the Ababa Institute on TV. The name rang a bell and I dug up the book and started again from page one. My leg was still giving me trouble, but my mind was *in readiness*. Someone had made notes in the margins, in handwriting so bad it might have been my own. I brought the book to my desk at Sempiternal, stealing glances throughout the day. It focused me during my solo lunches at the parklet across the road from the office. Honey mustard flecked the pages. I memorized Ababa's key points while on the phone with the Chicago branch. Pretty soon I was just staying home, copying out passages, taping them to the wall.

The things Ababa was saying were not for the timid, yet on the other hand they were for everyone. I read his other books, each one a straight-up life-changer, and it wasn't long before I paid a visit to the Ababa Institute in Hash Valley. They assigned me to Fritz, who had been in Iraq the first time around. We never even talked about what we'd seen, but everything he said made sense. How many people can you say that about? I tried to explain it to my dad once, but the Big Man wasn't having it. When Sempi's HR stooge called me at home to lower the boom, I just let it go to voicemail.

•

The steaks were in front of us, steaming visibly and branded with a grid so true it made me want to plot asymptotes. I couldn't bring the knife down. The steak was breathing, the knife was breathing. My father was scrutinizing his mashed potatoes, prepared to find fault. We sat, not talking, for approximately one hundred years.

"My tongue had to go to tongue school," Ababa writes, about the time an encounter with a lynx left him speechless.

The jukebox kicked in. Some song I used to hate, but at the moment it made me sad. It pinned me down. The roof workers from the motel were at the bar, drinking orange soda and eating chicken wings. A few of their friends had come along, too. Maybe they'd been working on the other side of the building, tossing ropes over the roof. Everyone was roughly the same size. I was blinking away a tear. I mean I blinked and a tear fell down.

"So." The Big Man put his hand on top of mine. It was like a sandbag falling.

"Yes?"

"You're fine, right?"

I was going to say yes but I didn't. I didn't know about fine. The concept needed to be explored. The weight of his hand trapped me, and the steak smell crowded my nose. I needed to erase the Big Man from the picture, catch my breath, for real. In a minute I saw myself as I was at Captain Clark's, schlepping my sign on that Thursday when I first meet Cyn. She looks frazzled but great. She's done that thing women do around the eyes. I guess it's called eye shadow. She looks part animal, feral, sexy. She has on these boots. I guess that's my type: part animal, boots.

"Can you help me?" she's saying. "Or are you just the end-of-the-line guy?"

"I'm more than that," I tell her. But am I? She explains the situation. The day before, she came to the store and bought those dental floss widgets, a refill of liquid soap, cough drops. She takes out the receipt, foreign in its crispness, like it's been dry-cleaned. The problem, she says, is that when she tried to refill her soap dispenser that morning, she couldn't find the shopping bag. She turned her apartment upside down, looking for her Captain Clark's purchases. Little do I know that this will soon be our apartment, that I'll come to love the way she loses things, car keys and house keys, entire bags of groceries. Love, or say I love.

She's sure she left the soap at the store, just paid and forgot it at the register. Yesterday, she remembers, she counted out exact change, $19.83, and maybe in her excitement she forgot to take what she'd come for in the first place. "I'm not always such an airhead," she says, showing her sharp, pretty teeth. "Just some weeks."

"It's a good number. It's the year I was born."

She looks up. "You're just a baby."

I keep focus on the wide sunglasses perched on her head. I can see myself curved in them, thin as a flame. I tell her I can help. I tell her to wait. I say it like I might be the manager. My leg is giving me all kinds of grief, but I grit my teeth and force a normal stride. I go up the stairs in the back and explain the situation to Ken. The receipt is time-stamped 2:55 on the afternoon of July 12, 2008.

"She a hottie?" he asks, cuing the closed-circuit from the day before.

"Ha, no." I watch the three screens, each capturing two registers. People move like robots.

"A babeski?"

"What? No."

Ken's aerie smells like socks, and there's always talk radio pouring from the small white German speakers. I hardly ever visit unless he tells me I messed up. Every so often I make a mistake, but I haven't made one in a while.

Ken used to make fun of my lisp but not anymore. He slows the video and there she is, gray and fuzzy and five times too small. You can't see her face, but it's definitely her. The hair, the boots, the shades. I could watch it the rest of the afternoon. I see her buy the soap and all the rest. I see her count out change, then answer her phone, then turn to leave, bag in hand.

It's like the first scene in a movie, I think. How will it end?

"Wow, she's super old," Ken says, pausing the feed. "I gotta use the can."

He disappears into the little bathroom. I sit with the frozen images, their edges shimmering, like a view of something deep under the sea. The radio show is on full blast, angry clowns who need to breathe better.

I go back downstairs and Cyn is sitting on a fake barrel that we sometimes put the cheese samples on, checking her phone or maybe just staring at her reflection. If I looked like she did, I would stare at myself all day. I take out three fives and four ones from my wallet, then three quarters, a nickel, and one, two, three pennies. I've always thought having exact change is good luck. I'm down to a buck and a quarter. There's more in the bank, but not much more. It doesn't matter.

"Here you go," I say. My feet get mixed up but she catches me, wedges her shoulder under my arm. The bills and the coins are still in my hand. I put the money in her purse and inhale silently, deeply. I wait for those pretty little teeth to show, knowing even then that it's the last time I'll do anything right.

SEVEN WOMEN

1.

Hannah Hahn was a legendary editor, though the reasons why were hard to pin down. She founded the literary journal *Hot Stanza* in 1989 out of her East Village studio. It ran for just four issues, two years between each, and the production values were practically nonexistent. Yet it was precisely this state of near absence that added luster to her myth. The submission process was at once straightforward and verging on the mystical. You'd send a twenty-page free-form rant to a P.O. box on Canal Street and a day or a year later Hannah would send you a typewritten postcard, having pruned your meanderings to three enigmatic sentences, one of which you never wrote. She'd also give it a new title, usually a number. Then she would reject it anyway.

To get rejected by Hannah Hahn was an achievement in itself. Writers pinned the postcards above their desks. An air of mystery hung over the proceedings. Hannah never went to parties, didn't own a phone. It was said she had a British accent, a harelip, a hearing aid, a stutter. A picture once circulated that some claimed showed Hannah emerging from a club called the Pyramid, looking like a cross between Bettie Page and Charles de Gaulle, but after a while this theory was discarded. Everyone expected her to be thinner, a hunger artist with Giacometti bones—a frame to match her pared-down aesthetic.

The last piece to appear in *Hot Stanza* was a lyric extracted from a radio weather report. It runs, in its entirety:

light rain touching parts of queens

2.

One of the handful of writers published in the pages of *Hot Stanza* is **Amanda Koo**, briefly known as Amadeus Ook, the drummer for Weird Menace. The name came from an old pulp magazine she found in a closet of the brownstone where she grew up, the literary residue of a former resident. She didn't read the stories, but the covers were all she needed.

The conceit behind her band was that its four members belonged to a cult that worshipped alien overlords, or that they were the alien overlords themselves—no one could keep the story straight. It's been said about the Velvet Underground that although only a few hundred people bought their first LP upon release, every one of them started a band; the joke about Weird Menace was that only twenty people ever heard them perform, but each one of them swore off music for life.

Now Amanda is a guidance counselor at Measures, a new private school built over a landfill in Upper Manhattan. The overlapping ovoid buildings look spun out of sugar, special glass that goes white in sunlight. When rain hits the façade it sets off a bouquet of harmonics, like an ambient steel-drum band at the most exclusive chill-out room on Ibiza. Inside are so-called learning pods that look like crumpled balls of paper, as if the architects had knocked over a trash can and said, *How about this?* Sometimes when she's talking to a student, listening to him drone on about lacrosse and string theory and some movie about 3D printers gone haywire, she gazes out the oddly shaped windows and loses her mind a little. Is the Band-Aid on the bridge of his nose legit or another bizarre fashion statement?

Or something *else*. In that moment she knows: the world has ended, the sun has died, and the student before her is some alien entity in a terrestrial sheath, draining her life force by the second.

3.

Escaped-animal Twitter handles: Could they be your legacy? Online, Amanda's daughter **Tina Koo** impersonates the mature Persian lynx that hopped the fence of a Fort Lauderdale menagerie. "Lynx hungry, lynx eat poodle." Stuff like that. Two days in and there are forty thousand followers. With the right weapons, you could overthrow a third-world government. Think of all the office time wasted, all across the country. The profile pic isn't of the lynx in question, just something Google spit up when she searched "lynx." Maybe it's not even a lynx. Perhaps just a very big house cat with fancy ears. You could argue that's part of the charm, the play between reality and fiction. But that doesn't explain forty thousand and climbing. Something is in the air, something desperate and a little depraved, held together by circuits and signals and stuffed up above in the cloud.

Adopted and Asian, a New Yorker born (she thinks) and bred, Tina had a kind of pre-midlife crisis and said goodbye to Amanda and all that paralyzing East Coast gravitas. She now lives outside Eucalyptus, California, where she surfs and tries to write screenplays. So far, nothing. Not nothing as in no bites from studio heads, but nothing as in no screenplays. The funny thing about writing is that it's hard. She thought surfing would inspire her, but it turns out all the surfing narratives have been done. It's not a sport that lends itself to layered storylines. "Surfing's over," another surfer, someone named Bronx, tells her, while proofing her latest inconclusive draft. It has major Act Two issues, and Act One is no cakewalk. It never gets to Act Three, but Tina is leaning toward having a shark eat most of the cast.

Bronx has some constructive criticism. "Change it to hockey and make all the characters chicks."

"What about the female characters?"

"Change them to dudes."

"And then what?"

But Bronx is already dissolving into the sun-blasted sea, just a set of shoulders now, or maybe those are waterbirds at rest in the glare. Tina turns back to her Twitter feed and types, "Just got great edits." Hashtag screenplay, hashtag lovemylife, hashtag killmenow. Would a lynx tweet this? Tina decides that *her* lynx would, and for some reason licks her lips.

4.

Before her untimely death, **Clyde Virtue,** née Fatkinson, lived a floor below Amanda Koo and her daughter, Tina, though Tina never knew her dramatically perfumed neighbor's name; she assumed the "Clyde" on the mailbox was a vestige of her late husband. After graduating Vassar, Clyde moved to Manhattan and through a series of frustrating jobs, before throwing herself to the gods of freelance reviewery. Fortunately, she wrote at breakneck speed, and with a high degree of style, and picked up work with seeming ease. However, even those closest to her, upon reading her pieces, would profess confusion as to what she thought of the work in question, be it a novel or opera or modernist office tower. She met with acclaim, and even attained a notoriety; a hit piece in *Spy* was headlined, "What Is She Thinking?" But Clyde quickly grew disillusioned with the *racket,* as she called it. Most disastrous, or amazing, depending on your stance, was when she tried her hand as a pop music critic, writing for a variety of places. Here it was perfectly obvious what she thought. Even though Clyde avoided contemporary music, if she could help it, she believed her ear to be infallible, for she knew the rudiments of music theory, and wrote forcibly about the dreck filling the airwaves. No band or movement was sacrosanct. She took pleasure in puncturing nostalgia acts and young Turks alike, indeed reserving particular venom for the Rod Stewart song "Young Turks." ("He sings that young *hearts* should run rampant tonight, as though he had quite forgotten his own title.") In her mind, the Beatles, a deeply flawed group at best, had clearly peaked with the soundtrack to *Help!,* and with the exception of a rare, practically unattainable Emmylou Harris demo, everything else since then was worthless, too. Indeed, practically every song ever recorded, not to mention the ones left unknown to posterity, was as offensive as could be imagined, and more than one of Clyde Fatkinson's reviews ended with some variation on the opinion that the consumer would do far better to seal up his ears with wax than to give the album in question even a single spin. Some editors who were entertained by Clyde's crankiness nevertheless feared for his sanity (they assumed the writer was a man) and figured his attitude was a result of him being more of a jazz or classical fan, and so tried to get him to switch his focus. But in truth she despised these forms even more. For Clyde Fatkinson, only the early compositions of John Philip Sousa, "an American master" in her words, bore repeated listenings.

Against all odds she fell in love with the producer Guy Virtue, whose musical flop *Burton!,* about the author of the seventeenth-century treatise *The Anatomy of Melancholy,* she panned in the pages of a stapled-together whatnot called *Hot Stanza*. Virtue agreed with her assessment; curious to meet her, he suggested lunch at his club, and the two were engaged, as they liked to tell it, *before dinner*.

5.

Down the hall from Clyde Virtue was a woman named **Klein.** We were neighborly, though for a long time I didn't know whether Klein was her first or last name. Early on she'd invited Ashley and me over for tea—"high tea," she called it, without irony, or perhaps with an irony so rarefied it eluded me. The talk was pleasant, though the tea was bad. Klein was well above six feet tall, diluted only slightly by her constant stoop. Afterward, Ashley and I estimated she could have been anywhere from four to fourteen years older than us, her skin smooth but her soft hair a uniform gray and worn like a helmet. She was Asian, like us; however, she never divulged any information that would shed light on her exact ethnicity or upbringing. Wherefore the single, non-Asiaphone moniker? Alas, it was not ours to fathom. Klein's place was the same size as ours yet felt at once more spacious, since she lived alone, and claustrophobic, as it appeared she never threw anything away. Everything was in its place: shoes in a shoe rack, hats neatly impaled on pegs, bills and papers stuffed in large boxes atop a long wooden desk. An assortment of keys hung from a series of cast-iron hooks near the entrance. Yet for all the visible organization, her quarters exuded the sensation of things about to burst at the seams. Floor-to-ceiling cases were crammed with books and old periodicals as fat as books, complete runs of bricklike journals with one-word titles like *Caesura* and *Embodiments,* and were notable for the absence of any sort of vase or picture frame or totemic tchotchke to break up the onslaught of spines. There was no breathing room. So tightly wedged together were the volumes that I was overcome with the frightening and delicious sense that if I were to attempt to pull one free, the whole shebang would come to grief. There would be no survivors. I had a fleeting presentiment of Klein's death by falling bookcase, her tall frame completely obscured, and undiscovered for weeks. The conversation eventually turned to telekinesis, flying saucers, continents lost to time and tide. Her tone remained jovial as she discussed these matters, considering the arguments pro and con in turn. Klein mentioned the neighbors in 1B, with the small children, and said that she would keep a casual eye on their growth, for a race of little people would foretell the apocalypse. She laughed as she said this. She spoke of alchemy, turning lead into gold. The alchemists yearned for immortal life, she said; what if one of them found it? He would still be alive today. But then wouldn't we know of his sustained existence? Ashley asked. At which Klein smiled and wondered if maybe a condition of such an extraordinary gift was that you could not broadcast it, you must keep it to yourself, be a creature of eternal anonymity. A month later, Klein invited us over again, to "chitchat about this and that." The tea was still bad. There was a plate of six Ritz crackers, with no cheese or other accompaniment. As though hypnotized, neither Ashley nor I partook of the snack, which might have been lying on the plate for hours if not weeks before our arrival. We talked about the mixed-up temperatures the city had experienced, which got Klein started on the history of climate prediction and weather control, in particular the "seeding" of clouds to create rain, and before long she was talking about actual cataclysmic meteorological events—earthquakes, floods—recorded across the ancient mythologies. She never got a third chance to invite us over, but we returned the favor and had Klein to our place for strudel and coffee. She didn't touch the latter but devoured the strudel, helping herself to seconds and in fact to thirds and technically fourths, fifths, and sixths, small irregular shapes that she carved with a strange precision. She seemed to swallow the pieces whole. She really did a job on that pastry. Ashley was amused, but I confess I was miffed about Klein's single-handed decimation of the strudel. I had wanted some more for myself. It had set me back $7.49 at Zabar's strudel counter. So strongly did I associate Klein with what amounted to a Sherman's March through that blessed confection that anytime I encountered her hence, the word "strudel" would flash in my mind, and though I don't claim to be a synesthete in my day-to-day life, the flavor of that distant afternoon's dessert would spring to my tongue. Relations cooled somewhat after that, though on one occasion, Ashley, on her own, ran into her on the sidewalk and treated her to an impromptu almond croissant and Pellegrino at a nearby upscale bakery. It was a Friday. Though only two or three years had passed since Strudelgate, Klein looked different, she said, now suddenly twenty or twenty-five years older than us, hair gone ghost white, eyes small and cloudy behind thick glasses. But the most startling thing was how large she had grown, boundaries shockingly extended, and her immense body was barely contained by her large black sacklike dress. Around her neck was a thin purple scarf, made of curiously tough material and tied in an elaborate fashion suggesting *quipu,* the cords used in ancient Inca knot writing. Even before they sat down, Klein mentioned that it had been a good day, that her entire week of stress and toil was worth it, for she had made stunning progress on her paragraph. Your *what*? Ashley asked, and ever civil, Klein explained. The paragraph was something she had been working on for five years now, on and off, mostly on, devoting her lunch break to its construction. Sometimes the work involved erasing what she had written the day before. Her labors had become legendary among the cognoscenti, or so she intimated. She refused to publish any portion of it until the entire thing was done. This heightened the anticipation among her literary friends. The work had taken its toll. Her body was in decline. Meals were frequently forgotten, or else in her single-minded pursuit of *le bon mot,* she would lose track of meals and eat breakfast twice, lunch from noon till four, and have an endless buffet for dinner. At one point, two years ago, the paragraph had dwindled to a single sentence, and a short one at that—a six-word truism that stole from her ex-husband's work. (A dark time, she said, a dark time, indeed.) Then she discovered "the key," as she called it, and the thing took on weight again. She bulked it out, bigger and better than before, she said. Ashley could tell that Klein wanted her to ask to read it, and Ashley *wanted* to ask; but she didn't really want to read it. Ashley's own job as a photographer's assistant left her feeling exhausted at day's end, and the only thing she wanted to do was curl up on the couch and watch bad TV until sleep overtook her. She hadn't read a book in years. We subscribed to a few magazines and got the Sunday *Times,* but I had only seen her glance at the front page; she never waded in. "*I* want to read it!" I told Ashley later. "I want to read the paragraph!" But though I visited Klein's apartment several times over the next few weeks, my knocks and notes went unanswered, and in early February the super told us that she had abruptly moved out just after Christmas.

6.

Dr. Emma Chew, Hannah Hahn's stepmother, was a revered psychoanalyst in her day. Once, when Hannah was young, she asked her what she did at work. "Sometimes people tell stories and they leave out the feelings," Dr. Chew informed her. "My job is to show them where the feelings are."

The good doctor hasn't practiced in years. I got to know her by sheer chance. One cold March morning, I was walking the short stretch of Eighty-third Street from Amsterdam to Broadway, where I would swing up to Eighty-sixth to catch the subway downtown. "Excuse me, young lady," a voice said. I turned to see an old woman, lost in a down coat so big it looked like a comforter. She smiled warmly, advancing her walker one slow square at a time along the icy pavement. The sunlight reflected off the parked cars stabbed my eyes. Where was she headed on this harsh day? "Do you want to hear a joke?"

As something of an amateur folklorist—I majored in oral history at Brown—I said, "Bring it on." Her face brightened. "There's a newly married couple," she said sweetly, breath making shapes in the air, "and they get along beautifully, except they always argue about how to fix breakfast. The husband works all day and thinks the wife should be the one making the meal. The wife knows herself to be incompetent in the kitchen, and besides, the husband's job is as a chef in one of the city's better dining establishments. Oh, the other thing I should mention is that the couple is quite religious—are you religious?"

I shook my head no.

"The husband—he is really a gorgeous man, very nice-looking, very virile—says to this wife one morning, 'I cook all day, the least you can do is bring me a cup of coffee.' The wife—she is also an attractive specimen—puts her foot down. She says, 'Darling, if you are truly pious, you will make the coffee. The Bible says it's the man's job.' 'That's ridiculous,' replies her husband. 'I've read the Bible from Genesis to Revelation and back, and I've never seen any commandment to that effect.' The wife, she smiles and pulls their trusty old Bible from the shelf above the toaster. She flips through the different books, Romans, Corinthians. Then she stops. 'See,' she says. 'He *brews*.'"

The old lady, who I would come to know as Dr. Emma Chew, MD, PhD, burst into laughter as we walked to the corner. "Do you get it?" she asked.

I told her I did.

7.

It's 1995. I am in Korea, where I've gone to lie low for a spell, hoping to escape all sorts of craziness, internal and ex-. But things are only getting more complicated and dangerous. I'm in a bad way, with options closing fast. In the mornings I run around a grim strip of park by the Han River. I take a shower while listening to the Armed Forces Korea Network.

No one can say my name here, *Miriam,* so I make up names. I tell people to call me whatever they want to call me.

I try to think of poems. Really scour that brain. What I get are stray lines that look like insane scraps of code. *Rain, heavy at times*. I fold them into squares and put them in my suit pockets, for later disbursement in the secret nooks of Seoul. There is no way to get back to me. I have hundreds of hidden readers, I tell myself. This is the means of publication.

Breakfast is a sweet bun bought the night before from the bakery down the block. Then I go into work, a forty-minute bus ride, with two changes, through sluggish traffic. Everyone has dust masks on. The air is particularly bad now. For the past few months, a grand old building from the '20s has been bashed and blasted, a relic of Japan's colonial past. I used to walk by that immensity, past policemen with machine guns who looked at me like I was a spy. I wasn't then, but now I am.

It will be years before the building is gone completely.

On this morning my satchel is heavier than usual. It contains a spiral-bound memo pad; a two-month-old issue of *Details* that my brother sent me from the States; an orange; my Walkman, holding a cassette of the Pet Shop Boys' *Behaviour;* a Signet Classics paperback of *Moby-Dick,* marked at Chapter 16 with a clean white feather I found in Apkujong; and a thin hardcover book in a plastic jacket, *Seven Women: Case Studies,* by Dr. Emma Chew, who of course I haven't met yet. I checked *Seven Women* out of the USIS library using my aunt's friend's card. I've only skimmed the first chapter, about an actress who starred in a string of B-movies before her rejection of acting as a "falseness upon a falseness"—the second falseness being life itself. Dr. Chew had a clear, often elegant style, and she thought up amusing pseudonyms for her patients, in this case "Suzanne O'Woe." Is it just coincidence (the good doctor wondered) that so many of Suzanne's roles involve a character bearing some wound from before the movie proper has begun—a dancer with a broken foot, an assassin missing two fingers, an archer with one eye?

But this morning I'm not in the mood for the doctor's spirited assessments. The book is dead weight. The strap I'm hanging from digs into my palm. The day ahead fills me with horror. The tasks; the filing; the attempts to use the fax; the mystery of what to eat for lunch. My position in this country is uncertain. There's a good chance I've done everything wrong. I study the passengers as they board, on the lookout for anything suspicious. I know the bus is a safe place to be, out in the open, but on this day it feels like a trap.

A polite voice asks me something. The speaker is a woman sitting next to the window. She's a little older than me, attractive and demure, wearing a soft green loden coat and white leather gloves. No dust mask. Her makeup is perfect, like she could step out onto the stage at the next stop. The pressures of the morning, the paranoia—all fall away. She smiles, and I realize she's finished asking her question. Her words make their way through my head for several moments, until the translation is complete, the meaning clear. Would I like her to hold my bag on her lap? Somehow this is even kinder than offering to give up her seat. I thank her, give a slight bow, and shake my head. I say in Korean, *I'm fine,* and for the rest of the ride at least, I am. When she leaves I give her the folded piece of paper from my pocket and say mysteriously, *Open it later*. I don't remember what it says, just know that I'll remember her the rest of my life. It's the last poem I ever write.

THE GIFT

Dear Alumni Notes,

We met as students of Dublinski, an eternity ago. The community college near the airport—who could guess the repercussions for the culture at large? Those were heady days. The campus rag had named Dublinski hottest prof three years running, and it was easy to see why, with his unshaven cosmopolitan allure and his elfin features and his endlessly repatched corduroy blazer. All swooned at a glimpse of that musty teal garment. But his class was not for the faint of heart. That semester, his Fundamentals of Aphorism lecture, which counted toward the communications major, had an enrollment of fifty—a figure halved, alas, by the second meeting. Only seven of us showed up the following week. The lecture was rebranded a seminar, now known as Advanced Aphorism. It would never be taught again.

For a long time we wondered what kind of suckers we were for staying. Dublinski would kick things off with an incomplete question. "Men are from Mars, women are from . . . ?" he'd say, and somehow you knew you weren't supposed to shout "Venus." Other times he proffered an ordinary, seemingly random phrase ("tennis balls"), or a guttural quasi-sound, a cough-hum or smack-sigh that would linger in our inner ears for ten seconds, twenty, a matter of immediate grave concern, until the classroom seemed wallpapered with its implications. It ate up the air. Assembled around the table, solemn as priests, we'd exchange glances that contained encyclopedias of meaning: a cry for help, take one for the team, come on *say* something.

At last some brave soul would lead the charge by repeating his words, if there had indeed been words, throwing in irrelevant new intonations ("Men *are* from Mars"). A fumbling for bearings, but it was a start. Someone else would chime in with an iffy clarification. A third would attempt a curveball, and then it was all we could do to keep our traps shut. Dublinski would swivel in his chair, directing conversational traffic with subtle tilts of his stubbly chin, while his fingers creased and uncreased a cigarette rolling paper. By the end of class it was reduced to a neat assortment of crumbs and worms, some inscrutable paper alphabet, which he'd leave for the janitor's broom.

Our chatter was ungainly, but we spoke from the heart. The ignorance on display was epic. We were not sophisticated. We'd barely survived high school. Books had never been our scene. Our scene was driving around, watching TV. Most of us had dumb part-time jobs, piercing ears at the Galleria, mopedding pizzas in boxes so big it was like delivering the Ten Commandments. But somehow Dublinski's supremely alien presence in our town spurred the seven of us to please him.

His origins were shrouded in rumor, perfumed with adventure and abstruse interlinear controversy. His native land no longer existed, someone said, its boundaries erased from all maps after decades of guerrilla warfare and bad architecture. Before coming to our minuscule school he'd held academic posts in five countries, on three continents, but we wanted Dublinski to like America—*our* version of America—the best. We had inherited the hospitality of our parents, who were mill workers and collision specialists, nurses eyeing retirement. We wanted to take him home and set him down to a gravied feast heavy on the spuds. We'd show him our collection of purloined road signs and pictures from the prom, or maybe just watch *Celebrity Jeopardy!* We wanted to explain the inner workings of local sports teams, tell him the best places for a haircut, hot dog, lube job. We wanted him to stay.

At times a pained look suffused Dublinski's face as he listened to our classroom ramblings, as if realizing that the eggplant fritters he'd carefully prepared for his mid-class snack were still on his kitchen counter. The only time he smiled was when the roar of an airplane, just launched or about to land, obliterated one of our wafty monologues. He'd pass a palm slowly over the top of his head, wiggling fingers in some foreign pantomime of flight, until the noise faded. Whoever had been speaking would get so distracted that when silence returned, the line of thought was never picked up again. In retrospect, this is what Dublinski was teaching us: to make every word count, attain maximum lexical density. You never knew when circumstances would cut things short.

There were no assignments. The syllabus instructed us to read Plato, the newspaper, and our favorite books from childhood. But none of these were ever discussed. When asked if we should be trying our hand at the form, honing our aphoristic skills for his review, Dublinski laughed so hard that the corners of his wise eyes glistened.

As the semester unwound, the class resembled a government in exile. It had no single physical home. It convened on Monday and Thursday evenings, at a location that changed depending on classroom availability. Our school had a modest student body but approximately five million committees and organizations, for everything from philately to step aerobics, the assault-awareness group Take Back the Night to Take Back the Knight, a chess mentoring program.

Might makes right. So it was that Dublinski's class was constantly being muscled out of the prime real estate by these clubs and forced into diminishing venues. The night of our final meeting, the entire campus was shut down due to some boiler-room fiasco. The outer doors were locked. Emergency floodlights made the campus bright as day. Dublinski brooded by the modernist statue in the quad, the thing that looked like a computer mouse giving birth to a U.K. voltage adapter.

Together we trekked across the snowy boulevard to P.S. 889. There, with a footpad's finesse, our leader slid a sleek black credit card to ease open a back door. We walked in the dark, through cold corridors smelling of pencils and lust, until we found a snug room with radiant heat.

We were even closer to the airport now, so that the arrivals and departures to and from our sad little city shook the plaster from the ceiling, to join the drifts on the floor. We tried not to inhale the flakes, which stuck in our scarves and eyelashes. By the end we resembled a band of polar explorers who had failed to reach their goal.

Then the miraculous occurred. As we shuffled out of the building, past the motivational posters and underpopulated trophy cases, Dublinski invited us to join him at a Chinese restaurant nearby. It was a stucco construction called Celestial Empire, where, after a jolt of plum wine, he started talking—saying more in one evening than he had in four months.

"All aphorisms," Dublinski declared that night, "hinge on their classification as such."

"Was *that* an aphorism?" one of us countered, in good humor.

"I'ma write that shit down," someone else said, whipping out a notebook.

Dublinski ignored our mirth. He speared a spring roll. "Further to the point," he continued, in his otherworldly English, "all *true* aphorisms aspire to anonymity. They are the gifts to civilization cleansed of ego. When you say to someone, 'That's the way the cookie crumbles,' it seems like the repetition of a cliché, but in fact it has value as the articulation of a truth."

"It's a cliché because it's true," one of us noted sagely.

To our surprise, Dublinski gave what most cultures would decode as a nod. "You could say that 'It's a cliché because it's true' is *itself* a cliché because it's true."

"Excuse me, Professor Dublinski?"

"Yes?"

"You're blowing our minds."

"Enough of that. Let us make room for the pu-pu platter. Please, eat. The pot stickers here are sublime. I have never tasted their like before."

We chewed and gulped in silence, stunned that the urbane Dublinski could praise anything in our rinky-dink town. To call it a cultural backwater was to be unfair to backwater.

"You all know Mercy Hospital downtown?" he asked. "They've been hurting financially for years. In comes Gordy Beaker, that self-styled nightlife entrepreneur who throws orgies in his mansion by the park." Dublinski was downright garrulous. "Beaker made his mint off a chain of strip clubs, some of the saddest in the hemisphere. Now, in a bid for respectability, he's waving millions in front of Mercy. The hospital wants to accept. His only condition is that they name the wing after him. Of course they will take the money, build the wing, memorialize this purveyor of sleaze."

We nodded blankly. What he'd said was too long to be an aphorism. Parable, maybe? Parable wasn't till next semester. Regardless, the fact that he knew anything about our civic life was a revelation.

"Most aphorisms are like that hospital wing. The provenance is rubbed in your face. The rank whiff of I-me-mine. The *true* aphorism is that which can be uttered and received with perfect grace. It is a gift no matter how many times it is spoken. The words float free of footnotes, their author unknown. Maybe he or she was a famous poet or the founder of a religion. Just as likely the words originated with a stevedore, a scullery maid, a peasant straining under the yoke."

Now all of us were taking notes. Dublinski was giving us the goods. The real deal. A waiter carved up Peking duck as we immortalized the moment. All of us were writing down "Peking duck," as if those words alone would be enough to conjure the scene, years into the future. And the truth is that they are.

"Every real aphorist knows that his best work is designed not only to survive him but to obliterate him," Dublinski said. "To be a sincere creator of aphorisms, one must of necessity become a ghost."

"What about Oscar Wilde?" we asked. "What about Heraclitus?"

"Talented hacks." He poured another round of tea, using the lazy Susan with brio. The ridges of his corduroy blazer rubbed against one another like rhythm from a mixing table.

"Consider our good friend Heraclitus. 'No man steps into the same river twice.' As an aphorism it approaches perfection. There is not a single person for whom that sentence does not resonate. But there's the nagging sense that we need to know who said it, and when, under what circumstances. True aphorism disdains not only its writer, but history itself."

Prawns appeared, and fearsome quantities of sea cucumber. There were plates of noodles and cans of Genesee beer.

"No man reads the same aphorism twice," one of us freestyled, and Dublinski cackled in delight. This was too much! Laughing at our jokes! We sat trembling, nerves aflame. The whole confusing semester was prelude to this evening, when all would be revealed.

By now the scant clientele had thinned. The workers were watching a spy movie on the black-and-white TV above the bar. Last call neared. On the small screen a masked assassin hamstered his way through the ventilation system. The picture went on the fritz as the door to Celestial Empire admitted a blast of icy wind. There stood a stout woman in a dark red parka, thick glasses, and a Medusan hat that turned out to be just her head, thick with frozen curls.

Dublinski cried out and rose to embrace her. They kissed each other three times per some ancient approved format, once on each cheek and a final swift brushing on the lips. He walked this formidable figure to our table, tucking her hand into the crook of his arm, and continued where he had left off. He offered no introduction. She pulled up a chair beside him and began draining his open beer.

We couldn't pay attention to a word Dublinski was saying. Who was she? His mother? His wife? An old friend, some fellow expat cast adrift in the icy American hinterland? She looked older by a decade or more. Vigorously, vaguely he nuzzled her neck.

Our conversation had derailed. The waiter relieved our agony by informing us that Celestial Empire was closing. We reached for our wallets but Dublinski's companion beat us to it, fanning five twenties on the table.

We opened our fortune cookies as we fetched our coats, which hung on a rack by the door.

" 'Love is like war: easy to begin but hard to stop.' "

" 'To know oneself, one should assert oneself.' "

" 'Traveling often is the key for health and happiness.' "

We'd all performed this ritual dozens of times before, but that night it was inscribed with fresh understanding. Freed from tawny shells, utterly disposable, forgotten except when some conjunction of phrasing and life caused them to lodge in the head: maybe these were in fact *true* aphorisms, of the sort Dublinski had spoken about.

One of us turned to him. "What does yours say?"

He looked at us, his seven faithful disciples. There was no way to know that this was the last time we'd see him. That his class, be it lecture or seminar or independent study, would not be listed in the spring catalog; that the dean of students would lie and say he was on sabbatical, when in fact he had been placed on administrative leave. That he was suspected of being drunk or deranged. That a strongly worded letter, typed on Kinko's finest bond and signed by the seven of us, would go unanswered. That Dublinski would vanish in a suspicious skiing accident—not in some crystalline European wonderland but on the chairlift at a tepid agglomeration of hills thirty miles south.

Twenty years have passed since that night at Celestial Empire. Now we have beards more salt than pepper, we have backaches and mortgages to moan about; we have lanky teenage spawn who say things like "Smell ya later" and advise us on which smartphones to buy, phones we're too scared to use. We have worked in advertising and the outer reaches of sales. We have been academics and housewives, journalists and Java programmers, vegetarians and slumlords. We have moved far away and stayed close to home. But as far as our paths have diverged, we have always been students of Dublinski.

Because on that evening, in the doorway of the Chinese restaurant, long since torn down for a parking lot of a gleaming superstore itself long since torn down, Dublinski's eyes filled with the serene glee of a hunter about to pull the trigger on a five-point buck. His right arm clutched his mysterious ample female, whom we were never able to track down—whose presence that evening some of us have recently begun to doubt. Was she some gauzy figure out of antiquity, the Spirit of Aphorism, who only materializes at moments of maximum import? He peered at the paper in his palm, already shredded to surds, and let his fortune fall to the floor.

In the manner of one giving a gift, Dublinski released the phrase that had either been curled up in his head for years or hidden in the fortune cookie just breached by his conquering thumb—that unimpeachable truth which two decades hence we encounter almost daily: on the phone with customer service and on the bleachers at Little League games; at business conferences in Hilton ballrooms and amid archaeological digs on tropical islands. How were we to know that we would hear it mouthed by our parents and lovers, electricians and mayors, our own therapists, for crying out loud? How were we to know that *we* would be the ones responsible for its inexorable spread?

For it was on that night, with the stars looking polished in the December sky, that Dublinski said, for the first time in recorded history, "It is—what it is."

Yours,

The Students of Dublinski

WATCH YOUR STEP

THE *ROBATAYAKI* BEGAN to fill as the snow came down in Itaewon. It looked pink outside. I'd been there since four, going over my notes to a story I had written. You could also say I'd been there since September. It doubled as my office and cafeteria. The waitress had kept me in squid crackers and Pocari Sweat, but real estate was getting scarce. It didn't matter that we'd slept together the week before, that she'd taught me new words I would never forget. She was twirling her pen. I needed to order something real or take a hike.

That's when I saw you, Chung, hustling in through the kitchen door. You always opted for the dramatic surreptitious entrance. You looked left, looked right, checked your hair in the dark gloss of an OB Golden Lager poster. You wore a thin black suit, gray shirt, no tie. You were the only Korean I knew with significant chest hair.

Anyone could tell you loved being a spy. I was also a spy, though you hadn't figured that out yet.

"I hoped I'd find you here," you said.

My waitress, all smiles once more, brought a bottle of soju and fired up the grill. "I should tell you that I'm waiting for someone," I lied.

"This will just take a minute. I need your help."

"I'm only good at crosswords," I said, brandishing my day-old *Herald Tribune*. "Spy stuff is hard, right?"

"Listen," you said. "This afternoon my uncle had me over for lunch." And soon you were telling me everything. That was the problem: you enjoyed the narrative of your own importance. It made you a charming conversationalist but a very bad spy.

We were playing for the same team, though every team had teams inside it. You didn't know any of this. You had hair on your chest and a terrific memory but poor judgment. You wouldn't last long.

"Once a month I go to Uncle's townhouse in Apkujong," you said. "His butler or whatever it's called in this country takes my coat. His chef, still haven't figured out if it's a dude or an *ajumma,* tells us the menu. Uncle and I stick to the normal topics. Weather, sports, my folks back in the States. The butler announces each dish as he brings it out. Four courses. French all the way. Uncle asks if I'm screwing anyone, offers to call this stewardess he knows."

"Can you get me her number?"

You laughed. You liked thinking of me as your lesbian sidekick, always armed with a quip. "It's the same ritual every month. We arrive at dessert. 'Decadent' doesn't begin to describe it. As I leave Uncle gives me a book with an American title. *Three Easy Rules for Impressing the Powers That Be: How to Win in the Workplace Every Damn Time*. Mercenary self-help, the kind of thing a businessman picks up at Kimpo as he's running to catch a flight to Delhi or Denver."

Your uncle had been one of the most corrupt members of the South Korean government during the '70s and '80s, which is saying something. He was retired but still a kingmaker, not just in politics but across the board: electronics, entertainment, academia. It didn't surprise me that he would help his nephew by slipping him state secrets and blackmail fodder, in exchange for crisp bills with perfect watermarks. He didn't need the money. It was a matter of principle. A whole philosophy. His corruption was so complete that for him *not* to do this would seem corrupt. I suppose you could call it a kind of purity.

"What do you do with the book?" I asked. "I didn't even know you could read Korean."

"The point of the book," you said, "isn't to *read* it. Remember, in the spy game, nothing is as it appears. The point is simply to look through it. Somewhere near the middle, a page will be missing. Let's say it's page 210. The next day, at 2:10 P.M., I go to the bookstore in the basement of the Kyobo Building and tell them that I'd like to return something. I show the woman at the information desk that there's a missing page. She gives me a fresh copy of the same book, assuring me that it's intact. She stamps the bottom edge with a little chop the size of a golf pencil. The catch is that it's *not* the same book—only the dust jacket is the same. What's inside is, let's just say, the information that my employers require."

You raised an eyebrow, and for a second I thought you knew who I was: not your friend but your minder. But the second passed, and I saw you for the fool you were.

"Then what do you do?" I asked. You demurred. A point in your favor. Of course I knew exactly what you did. You went to the Yonsei University Library and slipped the book into the Canadian literature section, three spaces from the end of the last shelf. My job was to swing by an hour later, scan the barcode, fax it back to your uncle from a secure Xerox shop in Dongdaemun. It was all a stupid loop. It was how we trained you amateurs.

≈

Chung, remember when we first met? We were passive-aggressive theater majors in college. Put two Koreans in a room of white people and they'll immediately assess each other for social status, accent, religious conviction. Impressions get formed in under a minute, then fossilize. You made a "wild guess" about my parents' schooling (SNU, Ewha) that was right on the money. I remember thinking, *Handsome trust-fund asshole* and turning away.

So it wasn't until after we ran into each other several years later, on a congested Myeongdong crosswalk, that I really got to know you. It was obvious you were trying to pick me up. When I made it clear I was off of guys, you were good with it, and I was your perfect audience. You liked talking to me because we came from similar American backgrounds, yet you were on the rise, in your element, whereas I was a nonentity: a struggling freelancer for the city's English-language papers. Closeted out of necessity. Your glitzy gig as a publicist for the Kim cartel's hottest soap stars, and your not-so-secret spywork, made your life seem the height of drama. I would get my kicks vicariously. Or so you thought.

For though it was true that I wrote for local rags—fluff about a new riverfront park, trends in canine fashion—these pieces were actually encoded with information about your activities. You could call what I did damage control. And you could call our meeting on that busy crosswalk, a year earlier, the beginning of my first assignment.

≈

The snow was unreal. The night was pink and pearl. The *robatayaki* was jammed, every table taken, and we had to share ours with two young lovelies still in office garb. I suggested that you and I retire to a *copybang* for cappuccino, my treat, but you warmed to your new potential audience. The women had apologized in fumbling English, their faces masks of polite incomprehension, but still. It was stupid to stay, Chung. I had grown to like you over the past year and didn't want to have you eliminated. I tried to think of reasons why you should live.

An Elvis Costello song came on the jukebox.

"What a horrible voice," you said. Right then I knew your days were numbered.

"Seriously," you said, digging your own grave, "who told him he could sing?"

I was diplomatic. "Elvis Costello is widely considered to be one of our most gifted songwriters."

"Yeah, well. He should leave the singing part to someone else." One of the women giggled. "Do you think he'd last a minute in Korea? They'd boo him before he left the dressing room. There's gifted and then there's gifted."

What did that even mean? At some point you had developed a knack for driving me up the wall.

My palm hurt. I realized I was making a fist under the table, digging my nails into myself. "Tell me about this lunch with your uncle."

You sighed, turned waxen. "I sensed something was wrong even before I went inside. There was a Lexus out front, driver asleep. No one met me at the door. I just walked in. Seated in the dining room was Johnny Oh."

"Johnny Oh?" I said. He was one of those people you always referred to by first and last name. "You mean from college?"

You nodded gravely. Johnny Oh was the third Korean American theater major at our school, the one who actually got all the roles. He played the Stage Manager in *Our Town* and Ivanov in *Ivanov*. He did a one-man show called *Papa,* conjuring a gruff Ernest Hemingway. Last I heard, he'd landed a speaking role on *Law & Order,* which wound up being cut. Still, it was pretty impressive.

"Johnny Oh is a spy," you said. "I knew it the second I saw him. He said, 'Chung, your uncle is indisposed, but he wants us to stay for lunch. Now that you're here, the chef can start bringing out the grub.' No hello, no long time no see. No explanation of why he was there.

"At that moment the butler came out of the kitchen, except he was dressed as the chef. He verified that my uncle was sick, but didn't elaborate. He said that it was good to see me again, after over a year. A year! I had just seen him a month ago. The way he said it put me on guard. I didn't know what was going on, but I knew discretion was key. For some reason, the butler was pretending to be the chef, and Johnny Oh didn't know the difference. My uncle was in danger—*that* much was clear."

"What did you and Johnny Oh talk about?"

You warmed to your tale. You were, I saw, well into your fourth beer. "I didn't want to press him about why he was at

Uncle's. I took it in stride. Acted bored. I asked him to fill me in on his thespian exploits. He said he was in Seoul to play the Korean American love interest in this new Shin Soo-il miniseries. The title in English is *Watch Your Step*." You plucked a Mild Seven from its pack and let it dangle from your lips, like you were waiting to be photographed. "What a fraud. I mean, Johnny Oh's Korean sucks more than mine."

"You don't speak *any* Korean," I said, fishing for a light.

"Precisely my point."

The women next to us perked up at the mention of Shin Soo-il, one of Asia's most watched actresses. You were oblivious.

"The really weird part was the food. The butler, now the chef, announced the first dish, something called chicken hash under nutmeg gratiné in sauce. It looked and tasted like plain yogurt with maybe a hint of spice. No chicken to speak of. And what sauce were they talking about? I'd never eaten anything this bland at Uncle's, ever. Not a leaf of kimchi in the place. It was the weirdest thing. And there was Johnny Oh, making a big show about how much he liked it."

"So it was bad?"

"I couldn't finish. Next dish was equally bizarre. Compote of marinated potato. First of all, Uncle *loathes* potatoes. What do you call them in Korean?"

"*Gamja*." A word every two-year-old knows.

"He's, like, *gamja*-phobic. Secondly, I don't think it even *was* potato, and there was nothing compote about it. It was more a thin, scalliony broth. The entrée was rice over miniature iced shrimp, which at least had some truth in advertising. Inedible. I was tempted to excuse myself, but Johnny Oh was staring at me, like he was waiting for me to make a wrong move. Like this was a test."

You took a drag. "I kept my cool. I said the lunch was certainly unusual. He had that goddamn smirk, you know the one, like when he did that dinner-theater production of *Nightmare on Elm Street*. Dessert was éclair donuts, which were essentially Boston cream pies. Go figure. Coffee wasn't even offered. It was just a weird and hostile vibe. The chef announcing every dish."

"Does the chef still print out a menu?"

"Every meal, man." You fished a card from an inside pocket.

MENU

CHICKEN HASH UNDER NUTMEG GRATINÉ IN SAUCE

COMPOTE OF MARINATED POTATO

RICE OVER MINIATURE ICED SHRIMP

ÉCLAIR DONUTS

"Can I keep this?"

"Knock yourself out, Miriam."

You shouldn't have said my name. I don't care if no one in the restaurant spoke English. You shouldn't have said my name.

"So you're saying it went well."

"It was a blast," you crowed. "Watching Johnny Oh watch me with his big famous-actor eyes. I could feel him wanting me to say I was impressed. Yeah, we'll see how well your little TV show does. I know for a fact that Shin can't stand him."

"Then what happened?"

"Nothing. It was time to go. Johnny Oh offered me a ride, but I caught a bus instead. I took it straight here."

"Why?" I asked.

"I want you to tell me what just happened, crossword lady," you said. "I think Uncle's in danger."

≈

Oh, Chung. You can't hear me now. You couldn't hear me then, or read my eyes, as the snow fell all over Itaewon, as the secretaries pushed off for the night, as we sampled every single flavor of soju, and I reassured you that Johnny Oh was harmless.

But you see, the minute you mentioned our classmate's name, I knew what he was doing in Seoul. There was no TV show. Johnny Oh was at the townhouse to make sure you were doing your job, that your uncle's natural affection for you wasn't endangering our operations. You'd managed the book drop-offs but hadn't been picking up the other signals. Worse, you were drawing attention to yourself, with your boasting and your chest hair.

Your uncle wasn't ill that day, and he wasn't in danger. He was in the kitchen with the chef, preparing the strange meals, giving them bogus names, hoping against hope you'd recognize what was happening: the so-called diner's cipher. You should have known this, but you didn't. You never were one for studying.

The diner's cipher? I'll spell it out for you, Chung. It was developed by U.S. intelligence in conjunction with army chefs during the Korean War. An impromptu maneuver—you can use any food you want. It's what you *call* the food that counts. Didn't you see the message embedded in the first letter of each word? I knew it from the very first course. "Chicken hash under nutmeg gratiné"? C, H, U, N, G. That spells "Chung," Chung. "In sauce" is I.S., *is*. I could see where this was going. A death sentence by way of the Cordon Bleu.

MENU

CHICKEN HASH UNDER NUTMEG GRATINÉ IN SAUCE

COMPOTE OF MARINATED POTATO

RICE OVER MINIATURE ICED SHRIMP

ÉCLAIR DONUTS

Chung is compromised.

You should have run, buddy boy. You should have left the country.

As we settled the bill, you said you'd go back to check on your uncle, make sure he was safe. Outside the *robatayaki* stood a family of knee-high snowmen—each made of two perfect spheres, equal in size. No middle. That's how Koreans do snowmen. The features were all twigs. Slit eyes made it look like they were sleeping, their smiles all serene. Straight lines, Chung. Straight lines and no middle and sweet dreams. That's how I do things, too.

You tried to hug one of them, but you were drunk and the head fell off. In your next life remember not to drink more than your companion. You forgot it that night with me. You forgot it on other nights, too, with other people—actresses and athletes, counterfeiters and counterspies. You shouldn't forget things like that.

The wind picked up. I stuffed you into a cab and gave the driver an address in Yeouido, the island in the middle of the Han. I brushed away a tear as the Hyundai sped off, slipping in the snow as it rounded the corner. You would arrive over water at an exact copy of your uncle's place, suspecting nothing. The menu slipped from my hand and I ground it into the wet pavement, mashed the black letters to nothing.

I took out a phone card and called the house, the replica.

Johnny Oh answered. He was doing Ivanov, with a little Freddy Krueger thrown in. He always had a taste for going over the edge, immersing himself in a role. There was a quality of violence that made his acting more authentic. But this was maybe his real voice after all. I didn't say my name. I was afraid of him, too. I just told him to expect some company.

TWO LAPTOPS

SOMETHING HAS CHANGED in my life. With my face, I should say. I don't know when it happened. My features look like they're slowly sliding off—some to the left, some to the right. Bits even seem to be heading north. It's not like I spend my days thinking about this unwelcome migration, but sometimes I'll see the change in a photograph, catch it in the mirror. In horror my face will scramble to right itself, the eyes moving back into place, the nose straightening, the lips losing their droop.

≈

But of course everything is changing. Cortright, my fourteen-year-old son, wants to become a rock star. He can't carry a tune and has no rhythm. He's tried to play guitar, keyboards, drums, trumpet, violin. He doesn't like being called Cortright anymore, or Cort. He hates his name and wants to be called C-Love. Better yet, he says, don't call me anything. He's a strange kid, but it could be worse.

≈

After my wife left me, I took a Mediterranean cruise by myself. It was unseasonably cold and I hardly left my cabin, even for meals. I had never been on a cruise before, but I thought that countering the dramatic change of Hannah's departure with another dramatic change—i.e., being at sea—was a good idea. Something along the lines of two wrongs making a right. It was a terrible idea. It was what it was.

≈

Hannah left me for Cortright's old piano teacher, a woman. I don't know how I feel about this. Well, I feel bad, but the precise nature of the badness is elusive. Had I been holding her back? Had Hannah always favored women, and if so, why had she agreed to get married in the first place? Maybe it meant that I had feminine qualities. I don't think I do, but it's possible.

"Let it go, Fritzie," she said, as she moved out the last of her things. I used to like it when she called me that, but I wasn't so sure now.

≈

I for one have felt some attraction for Cortright's former guitar instructor, also a woman, incidentally. I see her at the supermarket. She always wears an old tie-dyed shirt, the pattern in front like the Spiral Jetty. Her favorite group is Moby Grape. She's just over half my age but looks and moves like an old hippie.

≈

When it was clear that Cortright had no musical talent, we stopped the lessons. We thought maybe he would want to do sports instead. This was also a failure. One day he said he liked computers, so Hannah signed him up for a class at the community college by the airport. I gave him my old laptop. He mostly watches YouTube, teenagers covering songs he likes, shooting emotional glances into the laptop's pinprick lens.

Once when I was home sick from work I logged on and saw that he'd been leaving negative comments on these pining performances. By negative I mean nasty. There were acronyms I couldn't figure out and so I googled them. Then I wished I hadn't.

He was leaving them under the name CLove2012. This was back in 2010. It's 2011 now. Is something supposed to happen next year?

≈

Hannah and her companion live in the same condo development as me, Hash Valley Estates. In fact, they're more or less across the street, in the unit next to the one across from my building. They have no curtains. The angle is such that I can only see some of their furniture. When the lights are on. The lights aren't on all the time.

≈

It's not that I look every night. At first I did. I looked every hour. All I did was look. I rarely saw Hannah, but when I did I became all pulse and thought I'd faint. She looked so beautiful in this miniature form. Years had been taken off her age. Meanwhile my face was shifting, creeping out of symmetry.

I didn't know what to do. It all felt illegal and thrilling. Once Cort walked into the room while I was at the window, standing in my boxers.

"That's not Mom," he said. He switched off, living one day with his mother, one day with me.

"What?"

"Where you're looking. She's on the second floor."

The second floor was doused in drapes.

"Are you sure?"

"Those are the Chung-Ruizes. The mom is a doctor. I don't know what the dad is. A man of mystery."

"They have kids?"

"A little baby named Raoul."

"So I was spying on Dr. Chung-Ruiz. Does she look like Mom?"

"Not really," my son said.

I felt my face shift a little more.

≈

When Cortright—I'm sorry, I cannot call him C-Love—is staying with Hannah and the piano teacher, he brings his laptop with him. He has a small room there, filled with all the instruments he cannot play. Sometimes he'll Skype with me. The picture is unstable and the sound gets scratchy and so we hang up after a few minutes.

I don't know whether the problem is with their network or mine, or whether we're on the same network, or even really what a network is. But Cort's face will go metallic, bits of it gray and bits of it green. Big chunks of the image will fall out, so it looks like I'm seeing his skull.

At the same time, I know, I'm breaking up in front of his eyes. Although the way he describes it, it's just that the room I'm in is getting brighter and brighter until I disappear into the walls.

≈

Last night I came home from work and turned on the news. My son was already in his room, stereo on, lost in a stuttering beat that thumped from the speakers. I turned on the TV. I wanted to check email, even though I'd checked just before leaving my office at the Institute a half hour prior, not to mention on the way from the office to my car, twenty-five minutes earlier, and at every stoplight, and on the short walk from my garage to the door, three minutes ago.

This is my constant state. There's no one I'm expecting to hear from. I suppose I'm waiting to hear from someone I'm not expecting.

CNN hummed in the background, mixing with Cort's acid loops. I placed a frozen burrito into the microwave and entered a random unit of time. My computer was on now but it wasn't showing my usual desktop. I was looking into a space I'd never seen before. Hannah moved from one side of the screen to the other, disappearing as she exited each edge. She was saying something, but I couldn't hear. She didn't look particularly beautiful or luminous, different in any way. She didn't look happier or sadder. She looked absolutely the same. The top of the screen corroded, bits of gray and bits of green.

Cortright emerged from his lair and said he'd left his laptop at his mom's place, that he was going over to get it. I told him his dinner was in the microwave, he should eat before it got cold. I wanted to buy some more time, to look at Hannah exactly as she was. This was something I wouldn't be seeing again.

WEIRD MENACE

Oh, hello? Here we go! Hello there, and welcome, this is the commentary track to the collector's edition of *Weird Menace,* from 1975, excuse me, 1985, when I was just—well, I don't want to say how old, exactly! It is a "Blu-Screen," I am told by Tina, our producer.

A Blu-*ray,* rather.
I'm Barbara Lee Hanbok these days, but you probably know me as Baby Moran. Woo-hoo! Anyways, here I play a character named Lieutenant Carapace, who is a, well, you'll see.

And we have some nice music
here coming up under the
titles.

A shot of some stars. Galaxies.

Spinning, although rather
slowly, it must be said.

Do not adjust your set, ha.

A bit *too* slowly for my taste.

Makes you ponder your place
in the universe.

I should add that I never watch
my movies after they're
finished, so I'm not an
authority on the finer points of
the plot. Also it's been x
number of years, so.

Oh wait, that was just the
production company logo.

And I think we're frozen.

Well.

[*Whispers.*] Just talk? Sure.

[*Clears throat.*] For the past however many years I've been running a restaurant, Barbara's Steakhouse—come on by sometime. We're right on the border of West Eucalyptus and East Eucalyptus.

Not the best steak you've ever had, but definitely not the worst.

And—we have movement!

And over here in your right speaker—it's me, the director.

Ah!

Baby!

It's so good to *see* you! Hi!

They let you start this madness without me?

Tina said she couldn't wait and they'd dub you in later.

Say your name, doll.

This is Toner Low. I directed this piece of crap. [*Laughter.*]

Well, there's crap and then there's crap.

Speaking the truth. This is a good example of the latter. [*Laughter.*] Wait, which one is worse? [*Laughter.*] Set me straight here, Baby. [*Laughter.*]

"*Weird Menace* is on Broadway now, right?"
A musical.

Directed by what's his face.

I saw a picture of the actress who plays me.

Drop-dead gorgeous.

I believe it's called Photoshop. [*Laughter.*] You're a vision, Baby.

Well, *you* look fantastic, Toner, and you're sitting right here in the flesh.

Did you lose weight?

Not that I know of.

Practice your breathing?

Just the normal breathing. You know, the kind you need to stay alive.

Honestly, my ticker's not so hot. Doc says lay off the carbs and the

smoking and the whatnot. I eat celery and basically that's it. It's hardly a life.

Here we have a spaceship that looks like it's made from an old Mountain Dew bottle and some crepe paper.

Not too shabby.

Just got a card from Tina there, our producer, with one word on it: *Reminisce.*

I remember when you called to ask if I would play the role of Lieutenant Carapace. I was flattered but so confused.

Why confused?

You started telling me the plot and I couldn't keep it in my head.

Also it was four in the morning.

I have trouble with time zones.

We were in the same time zone.

Oh, that's right. [*Laughter.*]

Of course, when I realized it wasn't a dream, I was very touched. I had pretty much given up on movies, or the movies had given up on me. She said mournfully. [*Laughter.*]

I'd been such a huge fan of yours, Baby, ever since watching *Planet Zero* reruns as a kid.

That and *Castle Death*.

And *High Plains Succubus*.

And *Mephistopheles 2000*.

And the underrated *Suzanne O'Woe*.

Keep going. [*Laughter.*]

Here's a robot. Look at that thing go.

Crazy!

When I got the job, even though I knew you'd been out of the business for a while, I told the producer–

Hal Simmer, lovely man . . . such a huge—

What?

—*heart.*

[*Laughter.*] I told Simmer, I want Baby Moran in this picture. It's my first one, means a lot to me, please let me have her, one of the great overlooked talents, she's incredible.

What a charmer. You were what, twelve?

[*Laughter.*] Twenty, right.

Twenty-four going on sixty-five, it felt like. The story of how I got to helm this science-fiction extravaganza, *that* could fill a book.

We've got time, especially since, if memory serves, this transport-ship sequence lasts about thirteen hours. [*Laughter.*]

Basically about seven people had been hired and fired before me. I was literally working in the mailroom and Simmer was at wit's end. He came in cursing, kicked over a garbage can, and he said, "Find me a monkey to get this goddamn thing *done*."

Ha.

I happened to have a banana left over from lunch, so I started peeling it, making monkey sounds, jumping on the table and so forth. Simmer, he could *not* stop laughing. Rolling on the floor, swear to God. He hired me right then and there. He said, "This needs an overhaul," handed me the script. He said, "Finish it by the end of the day." Thank God he liked what I did.

That story's not even remotely true.

One thing led to another, and suddenly I have a chair with my name on the back of it. Misspelled, but it's the thought that counts. I insisted on getting you out of retirement. Simmer ran the numbers and said, "Go for it."

The robot appears to be sniffing a very long insole.

Ha, ha. Here's another robot—or, as they're called in *Weird Menace*, a "botkin." It's the same one as we used before, and we just added a nice green sheen in postproduction. To signify "radiation."

And here's that shot of the moon rising over Fibuna, the planet of many storms. Wait.

That's no moon, that's my *ass*!

I completely forgot about that shot.

Wow.

I don't know whether to apologize or hit Rewind.

What was the artistic reason for that, I'd like to know.

As a very old lady, I would like to formally thank you for including it.

Although wait. I'm not sure it's my butt.

We're talking nineteen seventy . . . nine?

Eighty-five, which would mean this was shot in nineteen eighty-four.

So definitely not my butt.

Nineteen seventy-nine, I thought, Well, there's a *chance*. [*Laughter.*]

Oh.

You're right. We used a body double.

It was Hannah.

Really—Hannah?

Yes, really Hannah. As in your *wife*.

Well, ex. And at the time we weren't married. Or were we. No. I met her on set. I know you know that. I'm explaining for the benefit of the viewer at home.

I've never seen someone so in love with another person.

?

I wasn't in love with her.

I meant she was in love with
you, doll.

**You can see why I hate myself,
right?**

You could have treated her a
little better, Toner.

Says the old hag who's been
married five times.

**We were only married three
months. A record.**

Not my place to criticize.
You're a sweetie.

Talk to me, Toner.

Okay, let's just watch for a
while.

Lost track—not sure what just
blew up, escape pod? Escaping
from what?

Some psychedelic mist right
here.

Okay.

And we are . . . high above another planet.

We forgot the caption.

Can we put a caption in, or does that ruin the integrity of the whole deal.

[*Muffled.*] Tina says yes we can.

This one looks like a beehive.

This is the first shot of you, Baby, playing Lieutenant Carapace of the 124th Interstellar Battalion.

Strutting my stuff.

Oh yeah. Come to Papa.

Seriously, actors walked differently back then. You could write a book—you could do a kick-ass five-hour documentary—on styles of cinematic walking over the decades. Now everyone just slouches and we're supposed to get excited.

These costumes are incredible.

Mark my words. This movie is prophetic. Right here: this is what the most elegant cyber-ladies will be wearing in the thirty-fourth century.

Who was the costume designer? Donna something.

She always wore funny earrings, like panda bears on acid one day, little blue iguanas the next.

I know who you're thinking of, yeah, blue iguanas. She was great. Had this great Bronx accent. Bronx or Brooklyn.

Donna Ignata? Ignatius? Igloo?

Ig is the right track. We can stalk her online later.

Ignacio? Who knows.

[*Wolf whistle.*] Hey, that's some futuristic cleavage.

Remember, folks, this is pre-Wonderbra.

Can't recall whether it was pre–plastic surgery, though. [*Laughter.*]

And another glimpse of Hannah.

Where?

Edge of the screen.

I'm going to let out an audible sigh. Ready?

There we go.

That was more like a moan.

It had to be done.

You okay?

My heart.

I'm fine.

Those of you at home, look at the right edge of the screen. There's a girl with her hair in sort of a modified beehive and very bright lipstick. That's the famous Hannah.

What a knockout. Even in the thirty-fourth century.

Hannah Hahn, ladies and gentlemen.

Maybe you at home will want to pause it right here and drink it in. That's fine.

We'll wait.

Moving right along.

If they've paused it, they can't
hear this part, right, Tania?
Sorry—*Tina*. Right?

You and Hannah don't talk, I
take it.

Email?

For those listening at home,
Toner is shaking his head,
pouring another drink.

One for me too, honey.

We used to see each other at
the Institute when I was in a
bad way.

She was there?

Yes—I mean, not like me. She
was working there.

With her husband at the time.

Husband.

He's a blur. A beige blur.

Tell me she didn't get ugly on me.

She was beautiful, Toner.

Oh.

Wish she weren't. Wish you'd said jowls and cottage-cheese thighs.

Haven't seen her in the flesh in forever.

Now it's just Facebook.

I never really check. I can check later if you want.

I have a personal page under my new name, and one for my restaurant.

Then there's a Baby Moran fan page that someone else set up.

Hannah's a friend on my personal page.

Hannah Hahn. Has a different last name now.

Happens to the best of us!

I remember the first time we met on set, they called her name, I said something like, "Hannah Hahn, how does it feel to be a palindrome?" And she was so sweet. She didn't tell me it wasn't a palindrome.

Palindromes are the ones that are the same forward and backward, right?

Hannah . . . Hahn.

Hannah.

Hahn.

She was a poet—I think she used to write poetry.

Or read it.

Here are the mutant attackers, the Zongans. I still don't understand *why* they mutated, what they mutated *from*, or, to be honest, what they're doing in the movie. They kind of disappear halfway through. You think it's going to be the Zongans versus the Terrans, which is to say, the Earth people, and then it's like, Hey, where'd you go?

My memory is that I wrote a more developed storyline involving Zongan gem mining, but Hal thought it was too political.

Lots of stuff got left out.

Luckily Blu-Ray has the director's cut.

Yes, but I never got to make one.

Then what is this?

[*Whispering.*] That Tina looks familiar.

Who?

The producer of this DVD. The one in the booth.

She kind of looks like Hannah.

I mean, what Hannah *used* to look like.

Did the dream sequence get cut?

Probably. Unless you consider the entire movie one long dream.

I confess that I don't.

Neither do I. But I find it can be a helpful way of looking at things. If you're trapped watching a particularly dire film, just tell yourself that one of the characters is having a bad dream.

Suddenly it all clicks and you are enjoying yourself. [*Laughter.*]

In our dreams everything is underlit and poorly acted. [*Laughter.*]

In our dreams no one knows what anyone is saying. The words are all wrong but the meanings are all right.

Wow.

I want that on my tombstone.

Are all those deleted scenes going to be special features for this disc?

God, I hope not.

The Zongans look pretty cool, all in all. From certain angles, under certain lighting. I like this main Zongan, Tuskus Madonga—no off-

color jokes, please—played by the late, great Sherman Battersea.

Poor Sherm. What a way to end a career. He studied at the Royal Shakespeare Academy.

Is that the name of the place? You always hear that about British actors. "So-and-so studied at the Royal Shakespeare Academy." Who knows if it's even true? But I'm sure Sherm was the real deal. Look at the thing he's doing with his chin. I could spend ten years trying to do it and still not come close.

What a total pro. I think it's *company*, the RSC.

He gets more mileage out of that chin dimple than most actors get with their entire body.

You could do a two-hour found-footage documentary about his chin dimple.

Sherm gave an interview right before he died, and he said that the most fun he had on-screen was playing the mutant prince.

He must have been out of his fucking mind. [*Laughter.*] But seriously, a real trooper. He was pretty hungover most of the time. I'm saying "trooper" with two *o*'s, but maybe it's supposed to be t-r-o-u-p-e-r, as in one who is part of a *troupe*.

The eternal question: Why is he the only mutant with a mustache?

Ha, ha. Good question. I don't know.

Because he's Tuskus Madonga, last prince of the Zongans!

It looks like a patch of seaweed that's been left to dry in the sun and then developed a will to power.

It is what it is.

The mustache was in his rider. [*Laughter.*]

The mustache had its own contract.

The mustache had its own *agent*.

That's *some* facial hair. Jesus.

I would not want to meet that mustache in a dark alley. Even with my training in Shotokan karate, which I picked up while preparing for *Dagger Dames,* a show that never came out.

And our helpful Tina has written on this card a question. . . . I'm getting pretty fond of these prompt cards, I don't know about you.

Anyway, the question reads, "Is there any truth to the rumor that Sherm needed the mustache because he was slated to play a Bond villain?"

The short or the long answer.

How about the long?

The long answer is no.

I remember this next shot, Toner. Two Zongans are

waiting to ambush me on the bridge, and—right here, see that foot sticking out, on the left? That's actually Hannah, she and I were talking, about you, actually, chatting away, girl talk, and it was this long tracking shot and I wasn't going to be in it till the end. Hannah and I got sort of lost in conversation and then I saw the camera and the boom rolling my way down the corridor and so I pushed her, you can see me push her! Well, if you rewind you can see me pushing something and you just see her foot. Then these two Zongans do their nonsense martial arts and pin me to the wall.

Ouch! I just felt the twinge again. Honestly, my elbow hasn't been the same since.

Oh, Baby. I'll buy you dinner after this and we'll call it square.

Please don't sue me. I don't have any money.

Okay. Dinner is on you.

Zongan martial arts, incidentally, combined jujitsu and something this homeless guy used to do every morning when he saw me walk by the office.

Finally seeing a little of the ice planet Tyo-Sen.

Featuring real ice cubes from the commissary.

Trying to remember why this movie was called *Weird Menace*. Don't tell me—I like being surprised. I hate spoilers, don't you? Yikes! That's some music!

We should check the levels on that. Some of the soundscapes in this picture are really great. Right now we're listening to the work of Bobby Delvish. Elvish?

Elvish Preshley.

Devlin? Bobby D. we called him. Did we call him that? Regardless,

we called him *something*. Great guy. Enormous cushion of a man, terrific mane of hair, like some medieval troubadour.

He always wore a beret, and he sounded like James Cagney on muscle relaxants. I'm not sure about the music right here, though. Talk about yikes. Laying it on a little thick there, Bobby. What I love is that he's singing in this language he invented just for the movie. Most people think it's Spanish, but it's Zongan, dammit.

God, this music is terrible. What, was there a fire sale on theremins?

Another drink?

You are an angel in human form, Baby.

Our viewers will probably be interested to know that we've been drinking this whole time. Did I already say this? Possibly.

Little itty-bitty drinklets.

Yep.

Yep.

Down the hatch.

I probably should know this, Baby. Were the Zongans helping the rebels or the good guys?

The rebels *were* the good guys.

Oh, right. Are you sure?

I mean, don't quote me.
[*Laughter.*]

What is . . . what is . . . going on . . . here.

I've neutralized one of the Zongans and I'm about to pitch the other one out the air lock. He goes whizzing like a Frisbee, if I remember correctly. There he goes.

No actual Frisbees were harmed in the making of this film.

The science behind this movie is utterly fascinating. [*Laughter.*] We had an astrophysicist from Caltech on retainer.

Was that the stoned guy who kept crying after every scene?

No, I'm pretty sure that was Hal Simmer's accountant.

Here's Tina again—hiya, sweetie. We're slightly sloshed. Tina just handed me a card with a question on it that I'm supposed to read. It says, "Where did the story come from?"

Like I said, I was just the rewrite monkey at first.

Complete with banana.

Exactly. Twenty years earlier—twenty!—someone had taken a stab at turning this long story from the fifties—a serialized novel—into a movie. About an interstellar empire, an uprising, and someone on Earth who keeps getting these messages about it, like news flashes, through the radio.

Very *War of the Worlds*.

Yeah, except it's just this one character, a Russian, who's hearing the news flashes. And he doesn't know if he's going mad or if he's become privy to some deep, dark secret.

The story was serialized in a magazine called *Weird Menace*—it ran a mix of pulpy old science fiction, horror, stuff with cults and conspiracies. Plus loose alien babes, who tended to show up on the cover. Anyway, that was the title that stuck, the title of the magazine. The guy who wrote the original screenplay was Gardner Graham or Gordon Gray, something like that. Gary Guggins. Nobody knows much about him. Just faded from the scene. Probably a pen name, my guess.

And there goes the other Zongan—bye-bye.

The script was about a man who steps inside a movie theater one afternoon, trying to break away from work for a while. The movie's about outer space, and he can't get back to the real world—like, he gets trapped in the movie. He finds himself on a planet, light-years from home. All he has are the clothes on his back, his wallet and keys. We get ten pages of his mental distress—no dialogue, just endless description of, like, the rocks and the wind. He's a complete wreck at first. He thinks of all the bad things he's done in his life, and how he deserves being stranded on this alien planet a thousand light-years from home.

Finally he gets his wits about him and prospers. He's a weakling compared to the natives, something to do with gravity. But then he finds this old music box that he can wind up with his house key, he discovers he can control the climate, do all this stuff. He's like a god. Who knows how that happens, but it is what it is.

He becomes a warlord of the planet, which is mostly tropical, palm trees. He subdues his enemies by freezing their lands in a perpetual winter, so they can't grow crops and so forth, and they become entirely subservient.

But there are rebellions, mutinies, and so our hero is constantly turning different portions of the planet into vast frozen wastes—it ends with the planet becoming a giant snowball, hurtling toward a black hole.

None of that's in *our* movie.

I'm totally shocked.

[*Laughter.*]

I'm just remembering the original ending. It's totally chilling.

He finally escapes the movie, or the planet—whichever. But his brain has become so scrambled that he goes on this horrible rampage, eventually gets shot by the police. And in his hand is just his house key.

Years pass, the script is forgotten, then Hal Simmer gets his hands on it, I don't know how. Mysterious woman made him an offer he couldn't refuse, is how he put it, but like I said, I don't know.

Mysterious how?

He said she had no face.

What?

That's what he said. She met him at a dive off Wilshire. She had on a trench coat with the collar turned up at a dive off Wilshire. Dark glasses and a scarf covering what was left. Like she was the Invisible Woman. She gave the impression she was Gordon's widow. Or daughter. Simmer was never sure. In any case, by the time I got my rewrite mitts on it, the premise was basically: frozen planet, people fighting, put in some spaceships, get out of the way. Oh, this is a great part:

that's Remy Fleeing-Cloud, the amazing Remy, playing the Zongan mind-jester.

"Methinks it a shame." Ha, ha! That became the running joke throughout the shoot.

He's like a classic Shakespearean "fool" figure.

That's not Remy.

Sure it is.

No, that's not Remy. It's Simmer's nephew or something. Bit part. Remy was in the implanted-memory scene. We haven't gotten to that part. I liked him. Very funny man but very odd. We all have our peculiarities. What in the world is *that*?

It's like a bagel they only make on special occasions.

The colors. Wow.

Is that a planet or a spaceship or a . . . oh, is it the creature that the Zongans conjure?

[*Laughter.*] I'm wondering the same thing myself. Also wondering if I should have watched this at least once before sitting down with you today. It's been years. I never saw it when it was in the theaters.

Neither did anyone else! And it was never on video, apparently.

Popped up on cable a couple times, as Tina informed me by writing on another of those little cards she keeps slipping to me.

The thing with me is, I've done so many movies, I can't even name them all . . .

Your fan club can.

Yes. I used to get the newsletter, very interesting. And then it stopped coming.

I think the fan club is still around. They've just gone underground

for a while. I let my membership lapse.

Well, maybe they'll be watching this. In any case, my point was that of all the movies I've been in, some good, some bad, I never thought *this* would be the one that stood the test of time. If it even does that. [*Laughter.*]

Don't mince words with me. [*Laughter.*]

What I mean is, there's no way I would have known that *this* would be the movie people got obsessed by. Obviously it's because there's now that video game. Which I haven't played but which I understand—correct me if I'm wrong—it doesn't have much to do with the movie. It's all about trying to find this magical pitchfork that belonged to Poseidon.

Pitchfork?

[*Laughter.*] Trident.

It's an ad for gum.

[*Laughter.*] But you're in the video game, aren't you?

Didn't you have to say the lines?

No, they sampled my voice from the movie and then they were able to make my character say whatever they wanted. Which is pretty creepy, really. I could be saying anything and I would have no idea.

Who knows if this is really me talking right now!

Here comes the meteor. We spray-painted a sponge and put it on top of a remote-control car. But the batteries were weak—that's why it's all wiggly.

It is not moving in a straight line.

Something to be said about imperfections.

Though I'm clearly not the one who's going to say it! [*Laughter.*]

There was actually this *band* called Weird Menace.

Someone sent me a tape.

You're pulling my leg.

Dead serious.

[*Laughter.*] *Why?*

The drummer sent me a tape a while ago. Never listened to it. We should put it on the soundtrack.

It can be a special feature, a bonus.

Like this commentary track. A little added value.

We'll ask Tania after the taping.

Tina.

Tina, I mean.

The idea here is that the metaphor—*meteor*, Christ!—the meteor is actually going to *save* the planet, not destroy it. But people think it needs to be stopped. That's why they're shooting all those missiles. Right?

Sure, sure.

Something like that. I knew the movie was confusing, but I guess I didn't think it was *this* confusing.

I'll come right out and say it: your script for *Weird Menace* was better than ninety-nine percent of the stuff you see that gets called good. It's too bad so much of what you shot had to be cut. I remember there was that love scene—we only got a snippet. Is it going to be included on the extras for the disc?

No idea.

You know the scene I'm talking about?

I don't think, no, I'm not sure.

The one with Hannah.

Where you volunteered to be Sherm's body double.

There were so many things that had to be cut. But I wasn't precious about them. This was my first movie. I was fine with cutting.

Or maybe you had your reasons.

Hal Simmer ran a tight ship. He was calling me first thing in the morning, last thing at night.

You could have fought a little
more, dug in your heels.

Easy to say that now.

Here's the guy whose job it is
to lure the metaphor to the
other planet.

Meteor.

That's what I said.

Nope.

What did I say?

Metaphor.

Sorry.

No sweat. Meteors *are* metaphors, at some level.

I mean, they must be, right?

There's crap and then there's crap. [*Laughter.*]

I don't know how we got this shot.

I think that's Hannah again.

Are you sure?

What's she doing?

I don't remember this, Toner.

Uh, is this the director's cut?

Do you recall this scene?

Wait.

This isn't—this isn't the movie anymore. It's something else.

I don't know how we got this shot.

This must be the scene, the full scene, the director's cut. Dug up from the vaults.

Clearly something's . . . yeah.

This is not anything I remember ever seeing.

But *I'm* the director, last I checked.

Huh.

Would you look. At. That.

Nicely shaped, I'll give you
that much.

PG-13? Should be PG-18, at
least.

PG-25. PG-36.

For mature audiences only.

PG-I don't know, 44, 53, 61?

Well, well. All right. Okay.
That's a lot of—yes.

Guess we should take five—eh,
Toner?

Hey. Are you . . .

Toner?

What's the name of the—
Tania? *Tania!* Tina, I mean.
Tina.

He's not— I can't feel
anything, I—

Toner? Are you okay? Are you
breathing—can you breathe,
Toner baby, say something—
say *something* to me.

Earth to Toner.

THOUGHT AND MEMORY

BACK IN 2008, when my first novel, *A Tree Grows in Baghdad,* came out, my publisher sent me on a nationwide tour. Sometimes folks showed up in droves, sometimes they didn't. It was great to see my public, regardless. I suppose I should say *the* public. Most hadn't read the book. And even though it was fiction, based more on stuff I'd heard about rather than experienced, I might as well have told all present that I'd written a memoir and that in the pages open before me, every vegan pita eaten, and every thought thought, was true. No one cared about the book, really, only about what I'd been through, and what my current position on the war was, and whether I wanted to go back.

The audience tended to be older. The men were what you'd call barrel-chested. The women, too.

I found I liked signing books, I mean the actual pen-meeting-paper part. I started appending a peace sign to my name. I must have shaken a thousand hands.

≈

By the end of the week, though, I was going a little crazy. In Seattle I woke up at six to do a live interview with a radio station in L.A.; but why six? The cities were in the same time zone.

It must be for a station no one listens to, I thought, and when I hung up the phone I wasn't convinced that an interview had in fact taken place. Had she really asked me about my health, my diet, my bad back? Had I really called my mother afterward, or simply dreamt it all? I've had dreams like that, where I think I wake up, but I'm still asleep. I've had dreams in which I slap the alarm clock, over and over again, until I'm finally sprung from the clutches of sleep, grateful and gasping for air.

≈

In Portland my handler, Jonas, took me to lunch at a locavore haunt that featured seafood haggis and artisanal jelly beans. He looked vaguely like me, the eyebrows and the ears. Over lunch he told me how Oregon was originally established as a whites-only state.

"O Negro," I blurted.

"What?"

"It's an anagram for Oregon."

"That's wild, man. I've lived here thirteen years and I never thought of that one. I guess that's why you're the writer."

We got in the car. Jonas regaled me with tales of other authors he'd escorted around town, dished about which ones were cool, which ones stuck-up, which ones needed to invest in deodorant. Then he asked if I wanted to play Ultimate Frisbee in the park with his friends. I was paranoid that this was some kind of test. If I said no, he'd tell the next novelist who passed through town what a conceited douchebag I was.

I pretended I hadn't heard him. On the radio they said that a science-fiction author named Vernon Bodily had died. He had written over a hundred novels.

"Well?" Jonas asked. "What do you say to some Ultimate?"

I mentioned my bad back, citing the dubious Los Angeles radio interview as evidence.

Jonas dropped me off at my hotel, where I tried to write a letter to this woman named Mercy Pang on the embossed stationery. The paper was so nice I got writer's block and took a three-hour nap. When I woke up I stared at the ceiling, wondering where I was. On the ceiling was a bright patch of overlapping circles, the reflection of water somewhere outside. I didn't recognize the enormous armchair across from me, or the ice bucket, the carpet, the drapes. There was no noise. It occurred to me that maybe it was 1979 and I was in the house where I grew up, lying on the sofa, imagining where I'd be in ten, then twenty, then thirty years. It was a game I used to play. Sometimes I'd think of a word or image and use my brain waves to send it to my future self. So was this me, sending a message backward to the boy I used to be? I wasn't even sure he was there anymore.

≈

In Berkeley I read at a transgender open mic at a bookstore that isn't one of those legendary Berkeley bookstores. It might not have technically been a bookstore. It looked more like a police station with a few shelves on the walls. I wasn't trans, alas, but maybe my publicist thought I was.

Mimi, the organizer, took the stage and introduced me. My name isn't hard to pronounce, but she mispronounced it. I instantly thought: *Canadian*. She looked like the kind of person who speaks English but whose every third thought is French.

The audience listened in polite if baffled silence as I read a selection from my book. It was about a team of art forgers who infiltrate the basement of a museum in Baghdad, intending to replace ancient Mesopotamian artifacts with cunning copies. They have come at a bad time. Fighting breaks out in the streets. Shells rock the building, and by the end they don't know which icons and ewers date from two millennia ago, and which were browned in an oven last week. They wind up leaving everything behind, the real and the false.

≈

Afterward, Mimi bought me a microbrew with runes on the label.

"Are you Canadian?" I asked.

"A lot of people think so," she said. "I guess it's because of the tattoo."

"What tattoo?"

She lifted her shirt and turned around. At first I thought it was a port-wine stain, but then I saw it was a maple leaf.

"I just like maple leaves," she said.

"Are you transgender?" I asked.

"Would you like me to be?"

I shrugged.

"I do have a glass eye," she said. "I don't know you well enough, and my hands are dirty. Otherwise, I'd take it out."

"Which one is glass?" We were staring at each other.

"Guess," she said.

"The left one."

"My left or your left?"

"Yours."

"Right."

"Right as in right or right as in correct?"

"Right as in right."

"Wait. So."

"Right."

"What?"

"Come here," she said.

≈

That night Mimi drove me to Los Angeles. She had to go anyway, she said. She'd taken her glass eye out and drove with a patch like a pirate. I should have offered to take the wheel but I've never learned stick. In the backseat was a huge birdcage in which her two pet crows, Thought and Memory, kept saying hello to each other. I don't mean hello in crow-speak, chirps and clucks, but "Hello" in English. They said it over and over, *Hello, hello*. They sounded like confused old men, happy to see each other again, even though they had just seen each other five seconds ago. The idea was that Mimi would drop the birds off with Harris, her nomad of a brother, who was in L.A. for a week. They'd been his to begin with.

"What does your brother do?" I asked.

"He's a science-fiction writer," she said.

"Have I heard of him?"

"Probably not. He's never published anything. Just some online fanfic."

"Did you hear that Vernon Bodily died?" I asked. "He wrote over a hundred books."

"There are about five that are any good," Mimi said, but she couldn't remember which ones. I watched the headlights carve the road out of the night. The radio was off, and in the backseat you could hear Thought and Memory sigh in their sleep, dreaming their way through a backlog of crow frustrations.

≈

My big L.A. reading got canceled. I went to the store, a place called Book Ark, a half hour early and the manager told me there'd been heavy water damage to the room, and that in any case the shipment of my books hadn't arrived. One excuse, and I would have believed him; two made it sound like a cover-up. The events organizer felt bad for me and said I could take any book I wanted as long as it wasn't an art book.

"No worries," I said. "I don't like art." I'm always saying things I don't mean, just to fill up silence. Then later I'll think that maybe I do mean them.

I went straight to science fiction and found the B's. There was a single thin Vernon Bodily title, with gaps around it suggesting that his death had driven sales. It was called *Handle with Care*.

I got a muffin from the café and then walked down to a record store in the same plaza. I didn't buy anything. I called Mimi, but she wasn't picking up. Her outgoing message was Thought and Memory saying "Hello."

"Hello," I said, talking to the crows more than to Mimi. "Goodbye."

≈

The next morning I took some stationery to the hotel pool. For the whole tour I'd been trying to write one lousy letter to Mercy Pang. I had four pages of false starts. She was in the middle of a six-week writers' retreat in North Dakota. There was no phone service, no internet. The only way to be in touch was by letter, and since I was traveling so much, it was my duty to keep her posted of my movements. But I couldn't think of much to say. We'd left things too ambiguous back East. There were no histrionics, just an email from her saying, "I think I like men."

The sun came out and I could see the wobbly net it made at the bottom of the pool, the light working through the water. I put that in the letter, then drew a big X across the paper. My false starts looked like they'd been written by someone else. I thought of just sending them to her, these abandoned epistles. Mercy knew all about giving up, and she was a certified expert in not even starting. She was the smartest person I knew, but she could never get anything done. She always claimed to be tired yet had trouble going to bed. Even sleep was a failure. At night she'd slip on the eye mask, plug her ears with foam bullets, and flip the white-noise machine to the highest setting. Still she'd toss like a captured trout, fidget, scratch.

In the pool someone was doing a splashless butterfly, lap after lap, so smoothly she, or possibly he, didn't seem human, more like part of some giant living clock. I took out a fresh piece of paper and wrote, "Dear Mercy," and left it at that.

≈

I was booked for a noon lunch interview with a reporter from the L.A. *Times*. I was supposed to go to a knishery called Barney Greengrass, an outpost of the famous Barney Greengrass in New York, which was on top of Barneys the department store, an outpost of the famous Barneys department store in New York. I waited for the reporter to show up. His or her name was Lane. Googling only turned up images of people Lane had profiled.

I sat down alone at last with my Vernon Bodily book, a trio

of novellas. In the first one a brave space explorer from the Terraplex, a gigantic floating city the size of a planet, is approaching the edge of the known universe. He has been on his journey for ten thousand years, having been frozen for most of it. Everyone he has ever loved has been dead for centuries. In ten minutes he will be crossing into an area completely beyond human and, for that matter, alien comprehension. He braces himself, closes his eyes. There's a sound like the bursting of a membrane. Then he looks at his scan-screen. His pyramid-shaped ship floats in brightness. Behind him is what appears to be a huge, lumpy beige package, a parcel of immense dimensions. He can see the star-shaped hole through which his spacecraft has exited. And below it, in letters of the Common Tongue somehow printed a mile high, are the words HANDLE WITH CARE.

≈

At three I got into a cab for LAX. My bags weighed a ton. Halfway to the airport, traffic came to a halt, as though a power blender had been switched off, so I made another go at writing a letter to Mercy. I told her about Seattle and Portland and Berkeley, about the transgender audience and the event organizer with the eye patch, the talking crows with the funny names. I told her about how hard it was not to lie during the Q&A, since many audience members assumed I'd fought in Iraq, when actually I was an embedded reporter—and not one of those grizzled journalists on a hard-hitting, truth-finding mission, but a freelancer for *Cigar Aficionado,* doing a think piece on the fate of the country's humidors. I wrote to Mercy about O Negro and the butterfly artist in the pool.

When I got to the end, I drew a peace sign. It was my best

one yet. I tilted my head back and looked out the window at the clouds. I had another moment where I thought back to being nine years old, sitting in my parents' station wagon on the way to violin camp, wondering where life would take me. It had taken me here. I was the same person, a body moving through time. Till what point? High above me two birds soared through the air, and though I knew they weren't Thought and Memory, I added a PS and put it in my letter that they were.

WELL-MOISTENED WITH CHEAP WINE, THE SAILOR AND THE WAYFARER SING OF THEIR ABSENT SWEETHEARTS

IT WAS GOOD where I was. I lived with seventeen beautiful, intelligent women, all named Tina, so I never got their names wrong. My name was also Tina, and it was pleasant to hear the chatter at dinner: "Tina, great job with the digging today," "Tina, you've done wonders with the jicama," "Tina, I have to say, those camouflage shorts are the shit." The self-reference *was* a little surreal at first, like someone was always talking about you, but we quickly came to relish the closed circuit of our situation. We wrote notes to each other that read like diary entries, all the most intimate things, ever so freely expressed. Dental floss and underwear were borrowed. Coming back from the dig site as the sky went sapphire, we would link arms and sing, till our lungs burned, the infinite glories of being Tina.

We had come to the island under the auspices of the Syllable Foundation. Our job was to gather and translate samples of the ancient writing known as oracle bone script. The island was lousy with it. OBS was a pictogrammic system of the early Shang dynasty that bore only a slight resemblance to modern Chinese. The name pretty much says it all. Three thousand years ago, priests would divine the future using turtle shells, dried bamboo, the shoulder blades of cattle. They would pose a question, then heat up the matter till it cracked. The answer lay in the breakage. Would tomorrow's hunt be successful? Would the rains fall soon? Was everybody really going to die?

They recorded the results right on the riven tabulae, with a proliferating vocabulary of symbols: a bolt of lightning, a labyrinth's futile curl, a vigilant eyeball, and dozens of other icons. To a degree these descriptions are Rorschach, yet one couldn't help but see in those jottings a pitchfork, or a cat's ears, or a horned head on a triangular body. (Indeed, the horns came up rather a lot.) Every few days we turned up a new symbol, and one of us would set to work teasing out its meaning. We tried to shed our modern sensibility, with consequently terse results. Even so, there was no guarantee that two of us would read the same line the same way.

This was abundantly clear from the first. Tina with the scorpion tattoo had unearthed a large clamshell spidered with cracks, on the underside of which were visible four characters. She propped it up on a dining table and got to work.

Horse

Run

Sun

Cave,

she wrote, in a lavish Spencerian hand. The marks were easy to identify. On the other side of the ledger, she inscribed her hypothesis: *When the cavalry flees the light of the sun, they live as if in a cave.* It was a little koan that slipped easily in and out of the mind.

After a lunch of champagne mangoes and eggs Benedict,

Tina, the one who wore her hair up in two "biscuits," studied the same row of markings. She tore a fresh sheet from the ledger, copied down the text, and wrote:

Storm

River

Dog

Spear.

"How . . . ?" sputtered the first Tina, rubbing her tattoo.

"Just because something *looks* like a horse's mane doesn't guarantee it means 'horse.' "

"But I'm basing it on the work of Klein at Yale and Dublinski at Penumbra."

"Klein and Dublinski have been obsolete for years," chimed in Tina, returning from the fields with berries in her calabash. "Besides, no one even *knew* about the island back then."

"So we start from scratch," said Hair-Biscuit Tina. "A storm. A river. A dog. A spear. I'm basing it on what we know today. I suggest you do the same."

The first Tina didn't seem upset, though her face registered perplexity. "You mean there was a storm, so they went to the river—and killed a dog with a spear?"

Tina with the French manicure spoke up: "Or do you mean that storms are like rivers, in that they bark like dogs?"

"You forgot the spear part," I said.

Hair-Biscuit Tina sighed. "Tina, Tina, think about it. You're living three thousand years ago. Everything is simple."

"But it can't just be things," complained Invisible Braces Tina, who I knew had written a monograph on either Dublinski or Klein. "There have to be *connections*."

All this philology was making us hungry. Tina with the perfect eyebrows spoke: "I want to make a pizza using pineapples and maybe some coconut."

"I second that emotion," said Tina.

I should mention that the island had no name, no human population apart from eighteen Tinas, and no fixed position: that is to say, it drifted in a rather astonishing rectangle two degrees longitude by a half degree latitude. Sometimes in bed you could feel the ground move, or convince yourself that you could. It did not appear on the normal maps. Tina suggested that we might be on one of the mythical islands that Qin Shi Huang, China's first emperor, believed was home to the elixir of immortality. Early in his reign he had sent his chief alchemist and a crew of a thousand virgins in search of it, but the ship never returned. I registered my skepticism: the water on the island was atrocious—an untreated pint would kill you—and the old quack probably had a different idea for the virgins. But Tina's romantic notion caught everyone's fancy: we would live forever, provided we stayed on the island. It would be our little Shangri-La.

As our term of contract passed the halfway mark, the happy mood darkened. We wanted never to leave, and came to dread the moment every morning when one of us had to flip the page on our communal calendar.

"What do you call Muhammad Ali after a bowl of beans?" Tina read aloud, to diffuse the gloom. It was one of those joke-a-day deals.

After a minute of stone silence, she tilted her head to read the inverted solution. "Gaseous Clay," she said. Someone started crying.

There was still so much to discover, so many characters left to translate. We wanted to extend our tour of duty. Tina suspected that the man who bankrolled the Syllable Foundation, an old China hand turned oil tycoon, had once pined for an unattainable Tina, perhaps had wooed her before the war and lost her when he came back limbless. Maybe he had dreamt her up while in the grips of malaria and never guessed her basic nonexistence. Such explanations were the stuff of florid fiction, and I tried to explain that it was just coincidence that out of three thousand applicants, the chosen ones all had the same name. But Tina and Tina and Tina weren't buying it.

We contemplated sending him some saucy photos, the Syllablic sybarites draped languorously over pottery shards and lexicons, feeding one another thumb-sized grapes, but that plan could backfire: it wouldn't do to waste a resource as precious as film. So we pecked out letters on the rusty old Remington, asking the Foundation to consider the value of establishing permanent scholars on the island. A final draft was produced. Then we realized there was no mail service. I volunteered to type out five more copies. These were sealed and tied to the legs of birds we'd befriended. We showed them a picture of our benefactor and hoped for the best, releasing them into the giant Rothko painting that was the sky at twilight, salmon over slate. The sight of those hearty messengers winging eastward filled our hearts with hope.

Later that night, after a rain had cleared the haze, with the moon dripping amber over everything, Tina noticed a few of the birds strutting outside the mess hall, looking a little sheepish, if that can be said of birds. They were pecking the dirt like chickens, trailing the letters they had ripped to shreds. It was too demoralizing for words. In our optimism we had sent off the originals, and none of us had the energy to re-create the language. Later Tina prepared a midnight snack, birds of paradise with peanut sauce, on skewers soaked in mint tea.

≈

We carried on. In the great cavern, atop wheeled scaffolding, we chalked up all the known symbols. It was a wall of text, massively beautiful, and the crude shapes seemed to hum with life. Each character was a meter high and numbered in red. On the opposite wall, on a more conservative scale, we wrote the corresponding definition or possible definitions. The rock turned pink with erasure and doubt.

It was hard work, and the idea of having a "personal life" was very alien indeed. Some Tinas had husbands; most had boyfriends; a few were looking extremely lesbian. I cannot deny a mad flirtation with Pageboy Tina, which faded as October rolled around. After a hard day's dig, we would swing in a single hammock, notebooks in hand and a head at either end, Englishing what we joked was the earliest love poetry extant. In the garden the deranged hydrangea bloomed backward, unfurling under Japanese lanterns and folding up like paper vampires at the first touch of dawn. All we knew were flowers and foot rubs and perfect acts of language. We listened as French Manicure Tina plucked her homemade cat-gut lute, and a chorus of Tinas resurrected a ramshackle sea chantey. I don't remember the words, just the diligent bees that coated the landscape, and the Venus flytraps snapping at the ghosts of bluebottles, and Tina disentangling forever her fingers from mine.

It was all over before it had even begun. One day I heard her tell Tina, in a voice designed for an audience, that she missed her fiancé, who sold stocks in San Diego, collected coins in Cap d'Antibes, played tight end in Tarrytown—I forget the specifics. *Fiancé my sculpted arse,* I thought. I was so confused. Love, if it was love, always kicked me in the teeth, even here among my supposed sisters. I told myself I wouldn't let Tina hurt me again, and later that night worked with renewed vigor on my character, the upside-down F.

I called it the Feather, partly for its shape, partly because the ivory sliver on which I'd found it looked like a quill. It was the only one of its kind. Its position amid a series of what we knew to be "placeholders"—they looked like asterisks—suggested a combination of the literal and the abstract. It was a tricky concept. A rendering of a hand, for example, could mean both an actual hand and associated activities: writing, hunting, cleaning, cooking. In certain cases, the definition of this same symbol went beyond that, to honesty (an open hand hides no weapons) or power (a mighty warrior needs no weapons to defeat a foe). When you got to that level, everything could mean anything, as well as its opposite. You had to pick which side of the contradiction to embrace, or else record the whole unholy snarl itself.

It was reasonable to link the Feather to an L-shaped letter, the meaning of which we had previously isolated as "singing" or "song." Tina had brilliantly noticed that it generally came before long descriptions of drinking. Furthermore, a small horizontal line, attached to the midpoint of stalk-based symbols and jutting right, was thought to denote incidents performed under some state of inebriation. Other rules and contexts presented themselves. With these in mind, I came up with "drink-song" as a definition for my Feather.

I said it aloud in my tent, long after midnight: "A drinking song? Maybe—not necessarily. You see, things were simple back then. You drank, you sang, but we cannot call it a drinking song, no, not yet. We need more pieces of the puzzle." I paced as I delivered my lecture extempore, in a German accent borrowed from my late mentor. In my mind the subtleties of the Feather became patent.

"Hello, darling," British Tina mumbled from her cot. "Could you put a lid on it, love?"

I pecked her on the cheek and snuffed the candle.

≈

The next morning brought applause at my solution, but also a fateful setback. Tina, who served up a mean Cobb salad, had fallen ill with a parasite. I touched the blue veins at her temple, not that I knew what I was doing, having lied about a nursing degree on my résumé. We loaded her and half a Virginia ham in a self-correcting canoe slathered with shark repellent. It would reach the mainland in a week. Tina, who had the best calligraphy, wrote detailed instructions as to the care our companion should receive.

Her replacement arrived twelve days later, in the same vessel. She introduced herself as Tina from Auckland and bore greetings from the Syllable Foundation. She had no discernible accent. We welcomed her with song and three long tables heaped with delicacies, though she only touched the melon and the wine. I held my tongue, but in truth, I suspected something from the moment I saw her leave the canoe and kick a donkey in the ribs. She was certainly a sight to behold. She had a potbelly and a John Wayne swagger and didn't care much for clothing. She was shorter than the average Tina by half a foot. When she removed her Stetson, we were greeted by a shock of powder-blue hair that looked like a chemistry and a physics experiment rolled into one.

That night I put my finger on it: she was a dead ringer for one of those little troll dolls that kids put on the ends of pencils. Who could forget their beady glare? I would call her Tina, but in my mind I prefixed an anagram. She was the Anti-Tina.

≈

Our curiously coiffed rookie bunked with "my" Tina, though of course I'd ceased to think of her that way. I noticed them walking to meals together, laughing in the stupid garden. They even did that tired routine: one would redden her lips with berries and drink from the chalice, then the other would sip from the same side and get the color smeared on.

Get a room, I thought, then realized they already shared one.

The week of the monsoon scare, all of us moved our tents to the cavern. We piled stones by the entrance and hunkered down, taking an impromptu vacation, but the Anti-Tina braved the weather, disappearing for hours. One morning I saw her head off to the dig site alone. I took an alternate route and met her there, feigning surprise and (what was harder) delight.

"Brilliant work on the 'Feather,'" she said, in her evil chipper voice.

"Thanks. It was hard work."

"Translation always is. Of course it's completely wrong."

Though I had no reason not to expect animosity, the words felt like a slap. "Is it."

"You isolated the radical for 'drink' and the radical for 'song' and you got 'drink-song.' That's hardly what I'd call poetic."

"Poetry's not the point," I said. I questioned her anachronistic use of the word "radical" but held my tongue. "We're committed to accuracy."

"All poetry is accuracy," she said.

I was regretting my decision to trail her. "Who died and made you goddess?" I muttered.

"Your so-called Feather really unfolds like so." She held up a finger and translated, in a warbly voice a half octave higher than her normal one:

> "Well-moistened with cheap wine,
> The sailor and the wayfarer
> Sing of their absent sweethearts!"

I burst out laughing. "Sure, sure. That'll go over great with the rest of the Tinas."

"Amateurs," she snorted. "Tell me, Tina. What do you know about the Shang dynasty? What do you *really* know?"

I didn't answer. She unscrewed a flask and took a swig.

"You studied with Professor Mütter at Princeton, right?"

"That's the other Tina. I was at Michigan."

"Ah. With Dickie Phung and that wretched Ledbetter."

"I won't listen to you insult my mentors," I said. I walked off, but the Anti-Tina kept pace beside me, whiskey on her breath.

"There *was* no Shang dynasty," she said. "You know that it was pure myth until 1899, right? It was like believing in Zeus. Then a professor, bumbling around in the boondocks, went to fill a prescription and saw these grotty turtle shells in the window, covered with weird letters." I knew the story, but I let the troll finish. "The country folk had used this stuff for medicine, grinding it up, mixing it with water and mushrooms. And then—wham. Suddenly all the gobbledygook was supposed to be writing from the Shang dynasty."

"You're saying it's not writing, just nonsense pictures?"

The Anti-Tina shook her head. "Thing is, you've got it all wrong on the level of *history*." She picked up a stick and started peeling off the bark. "Did you ever hear of the Kingdom of Women?"

"Can't say I have."

"An old wives' tale, a land of Chinese amazons. Sailors supposedly reached it in the fifth century. Some say it might have been America. But that's wrong. It was here. On this island." She threw the stick back into the brush. "And we weren't even Chinese."

I stopped. What did she mean, "we"?

"It was beautiful, it was beautiful for a thousand years, we had no weapons or war, we had plenty to eat, we lived till a hundred or more," she babbled. "Each letter had a meaning and each person was a letter, and when somebody said your letter aloud you had to go to them. Even if you were sick, or dying, or dead." She put a hand on my arm. "Which is why I'm here, Tina. Your 'Feather' was *my* letter."

I felt dizzy. I wondered, for the first real time, whether the Syllable Foundation had actually sent her—or if she'd ambushed our poor, parasite-prone Tina. We should have never let her go off alone. Sharks hadn't been the worst of it.

The Anti-Tina continued to talk: "We imported men from the mainland and fed them black porridge to forget, and once they'd served their purpose we sent them back." She paused. "Baby boys we left for the turtles and the lyrebirds."

"And you all had blue hair," I said. "Okay."

"That's right! And we all had something else." She tipped her head forward, gathering thick strands with either hand, until I could see two dark little horns. When I awoke I was alone, at the temple ruins, two miles from camp, with a blanket wrapped around me and a log under my head.

≈

I didn't mention the horns the next day, or the next; in time I wondered whether I had dreamt it all. The Anti-Tina now wore her Stetson round the clock and was definitely avoiding me, while bonding with the others. Her saccharine voice, her fake hearty laugh. It was like she was running for sheriff.

On the first day of November, French Manicure Tina was hunting a rabbit on foot—using the ineffective method of throwing pebbles—when she found herself by a creek bed that had eluded our mapping. Something on a flat rock caught the sun, and when she waded in she discovered a knot of gold as big as her hand.

"Gold!" Tina cried. "Gold!"

And like lemmings, the rest of the Tinas rushed to the water. Tina left the leeks on the chopping board and brought pans and Tupperware from the cupboards. Hair-Biscuit Tina, the most accomplished scholar I'd ever met, stopped translating a segment of turtle shell to run barefoot and screaming with joy.

The gleam from the creek was unreal. You couldn't tell where the sun left off and the gold began. Everyone was panning, dancing, even crying. But where was the Anti-Tina? Something was wrong. I sensed her spying from the margins with a glass, gauging how easy it would be to claim us, an army of Tinas already in love with her. I began to shout, telling everyone to stop, that we weren't here for treasure, that we shouldn't be putting a price on our souls. Then I tripped on a hunk of gold. They dragged me back to camp, and Hypodermic Tina slipped me a sedative that collapsed the hours.

"Tina, are you feeling okay?" It was my ex, good old Tina with the fiancé, close enough to kiss.

"Couldn't be better. It's the rest of you I'm worried about."

The whole thing was maddening. They were still blind to the setup, and the more I inveighed, the less they wanted anything to do with me. I knew if I dug under the Anti-Tina's cot, I would find bars of gold, with tools to forge them into "natural" shapes. I would find blue dye, glue-on horns, and who knew what other jiggery-pokery. There would be an elaborate headdress, made of conch shells and jade, for whenever she crowned herself queen of the Kingdom of Women.

All the Tinas loved her and now most thought I was nuts. That night I packed silently. I patted my bunkmate Tina's beautiful blond hair, the edges of which, I noticed, had gone turquoise. An unchecked tear rolled off my cheek onto hers.

"You're off then, love," she said, between snores. "Mind the gap, as they say. Mind the gap."

≈

When the canoe hits the mainland the dockworkers ask me where I've come from, in a derelict dialect that's hard to sort out. I say nothing and hand over my notebook full of oracles. At town hall I down a thimble of rice wine and ring up the Syllable Foundation. The connection is surprisingly clear. The woman who answers the phone, to my relief, is not named Tina. I tell Rachel that the island has been swallowed up, that all you can see from above is a widening mass the color of ink. I use the phrase "only survivor."

Rachel spells out the password for my plane ticket, which will be waiting for me at the Shanghai airport. I try to sleep on the train. Even the racket of the wheels can't muffle the voices from the shore. They repeat my name so many times that it breaks the consonant fetters, merges with the songs of birds whose names I never learned. Now I can see the Tinas holding up their gold-grubbing pans, standing tall and tan in panama hats, bandanna bikinis. The river shimmers like a special effect.

Standing alone on a shelf in the cliff wall, the Anti-Tina surveys their work, their hair. Her horns are in the open. She sees my vessel and waves with one hand, drinking the last of the year's good wine with the other. The wind is a cat's paw, conjuring a rune on the water, two lines crossing at a slant. My oracle book is gone, and I try to remember the meaning. It might be as long as the tale I've just told or as short as a single word: *Go,* I think it means, or *stay*. Or possibly both at once.

EAT PRAY CLICK

MANY WOULD HACK the Kindle after Rolph, of course, but to frivolous ends. As we all know, malicious teens from Mumbai to Milwaukee have since implanted viruses that the unwitting reader downloads along with her paperless copy of *Eat Pray Love*. Animated scorpions run amok across *The Corrections;* the text of *The Glass Castle* turns Swedish in the middle of chapter three. Patches get issued. The trouble stops. But Rolph's masterpiece lives on and on.

≈

Rolph and I were in a fiction workshop with Stoops back in college—Stoops was all but forgotten then, despite having singlehandedly founded Sensibilism in the '70s and its antithesis, Mood Writing, in the late '80s. Rolph was the star of our class; I was a satellite, a speck. I realized my lack of talent early and shook off the scribbling bug. Eventually I got into detective work.

Rolph kept at it. He had huge ambitions for his novel, or novels—it was hard to tell whether he was working on one immense story, a ten-volume roman-fleuve. Every time I called, he would be in the middle of a sentence or just about to revise a dream sequence or tuckered out after a day of research.

≈

We both landed in Brooklyn in the late '90s. Despite living a few blocks from each other, we rarely met. We kept in touch by post, like men of letters from another era, signing our missives "As ever" or "What larks!" or "Yr Humble Obd't Servant." We would have used telegrams, had they still been around, or carrier pigeons. He wrote very little about himself, instead using me as a sounding board for his great secret work, the Novel or Novels, tentatively titled *The Dizzies* but pronounced "The Disease." That was the kind of writer he was—pure Sensibilism, with a shot of Mood Writing. Old Stoops would have been proud.

≈

Excerpts appeared in hard-to-find publications, from the biannual Southern-lit anthology *Hot Gumbo* to *Fungus #4*, the farewell issue. (An appallingly high percentage of these titles went defunct soon after publishing Rolph.) Every selection I came across was brilliant . . . and completely unlike any other part I'd seen. I had no idea how it would all hang together, even though I was privy to Rolph's obscure architectural strategies and what he called his "ongoing hissy fit aimed at traditional narrative." Basically, he longed for a text that wasn't set in stone, something more akin to a living organism—a story with free will. He didn't like that books started on the first page and ended on the last.

"Where's the freedom in that?" he'd say, in letter after letter.

He joked that the right way to read an obituary was from the final paragraph back up to the lede, or that most books are better if you dive in at page ninety-nine. At least I *thought* he was joking.

Complaining about pagination seemed fruitless to me, if not insane. But eventually the intimate, hectoring tone of his letters worked its magic, and I found myself agreeing. "Books bore me these days," I'd reply, and he'd quickly, merrily attribute my ennui to the limits of the printed page. Then I started to believe myself. I stopped reading books, which felt flat and overdetermined. I concentrated on my detective work. Tracing the paths of scurrilous lovers. Working that telephoto lens.

≈

I don't know how he found time to write. By profession, Rolph was an ethical hacker. As he explained it, he thought like a bad guy in order to erect firewalls, stump spammers, maximize password protection. In the early days, his calling card was a virus he designed that, if unleashed, turned every bit of text on the victim's hard drive into one long, unpunctuated sentence that unfurled at the bottom of the screen like a stock ticker. He would send it to a company's president, with an explanatory note and an anonymous, untraceable email address. An offer of employment generally came within the hour. He was doing them a favor, and you couldn't really call it extortion, right? Citing my professional expertise, I assured him he was in the clear. I had no idea what I was talking about.

≈

One winter in the early aughts, we bumped into each other on my street in the shallows of Bushwick. He nodded me into a Chinese restaurant, though that is a glorified term. It was one of those places with bulletproof glass, garishly backlit shots of noodle options like autopsy photos, and three flaking tables bolted to the tiled floor. "We can talk here." Over egg foo young so bad it was practically mythical, I asked him about *The Diz-*

zies. Nearly a year had passed since the last excerpt surfaced—but he just grinned and pulled something out of his messenger bag. "This is even better," he said.

≈

It appeared to be a large plank of designer chocolate, still wrapped in foil, the kind he used to nibble on in Stoops's workshop. Peeling back the shiny shroud revealed a milk-beige rectangle with soft stains on it. *Words*. He pressed the left margin, and I saw "pages" of *The Catcher in the Rye* evaporate and resolve. It was a prototype, he said, of something called the Kindle.

Rolph had been "out west" for a while. Having caught wind of plans for the Kindle long ago, he'd offered his services to the powers that be, doubtless having sent some version of his Molly Bloomian calling card. In short order, he was hired to work on the new device.

Removing the last of the foil revealed a first-generation iPod, corded to the Kindle like a stalwart lifeboat. On it were small text files drawn from the works of Raymond Carver and John Irving, Salinger and Vonnegut. Rolph palpated the click wheel, pressed another of the long, thin buttons on the edge of the Kindle, and told me to read the page again. It was the scene where Holden's wondering where the Central Park ducks go in the winter, except now (click) the narrator is drawing a cathedral with a blind man, or (spin, click) wrestling with a cross-dressing bear, or (spin, click, click) memorializing the fire-bombing of Dresden.

≈

The demonstration could not fail to impress, though I didn't grasp why anyone would want to do that to their books. Rolph explained what he had in mind: rather than buy a single, static reading experience, the customer would purchase a fluctuating, *organic* story. His overlords initially swooned to his utopian tune, but soon balked at the logistics. What author would want to generate all this new "potential" content? A book (decreed those ignorant, illiterate *fools*) has a beginning, a middle, and an end, not several dozen of each. They had invented a device packed with possibility, Rolph conceded, a vast improvement over the traditional paste-and-paper book. But the technology was going to be wasted. "A whole new way of reading," Rolph said, "and all they want to do is play it safe." We said goodbye, made noises about keeping in touch, and never saw each other again.

≈

That's not entirely true. On a Christmas Eve ten years ago, taking a break from a thorny case of identity theft, I was hailed to my study by what sounded like the bell of an old-fashioned phone: Rolph was trying to Skype me. "I'm at a diner in Fort Greene," said the blurry, Rolph-like lump. "I didn't tell you everything." He picked up where our earlier conversation left off, years before.

"Imagine that the book is changing *as* you read it—that the next chapter will be altered based on what the Kindle thinks is good for you. Hear me out. The first time you take a break and power down the device, it actually stays awake and gets to work. It contemplates your rate of virtual page turns, the enthusiastic heat from your thumbs. If it senses that you're the kind of person who can't wait, and that you intend to read a good chunk of the book *right now,* it will make certain reasonable assumptions about your reading tastes, and then access Update A, which contains subtle changes to the original. A few of the tertiary players might be given bigger speaking roles, while some of the main characters futz around in a beach house, away from the action.

"If you are *not* particularly engaged with the book, indeed if it seems you're in danger of abandoning it, more dramatic events get inserted. Here comes Update B. Now, as you turn the virtual page, a mysterious letter lands on the heroine's desk, and someone claiming to be a long-lost cousin is on the phone with urgent, inscrutable news. The house next door is haunted. War is declared. The slumbering volcano comes to life.

"*Those* chapters will arrive within minutes. The device will place them at key points in the storyline, though you, the reader, don't know this. Let's say that you finally fall asleep after a long night of reading. Before dawn, the book regenerates. It loads Update C, Update X, Update L-33. Evocative adjectives that you enjoyed the first time around now unfold into elaborate metaphors. New connections are made. The story has undergone a hundred revisions—a hundred improvements—since you first turned it on."

"But what if you read the book again?" I asked. "What if you want to read the same story twice?"

"We both know that's impossible, even with static books. With a Kindle text, the second time around is even more revelatory than the first. You *think* you know what's going to happen, but there are bold twists, fresh omissions. Chapter twelve gets dropped—you won't realize this gap till much later, upon finishing chapter twenty and savoring a fresh description of the hairs on a waitress's arms . . . and realizing that this *must* be the same woman who applied for the temp job back in chapter twelve.

You flip back, using the arrow buttons, to check, and chapter twelve is in fact what chapter thirteen used to be, and there *is* no scene at a temp agency, well, no scene that you can find. . . ."

The Rolph blob quivered, the audio turned to a harsh screech, and I feared the connection would be lost. Half a minute passed before things stabilized. I caught Rolph in midsentence, telling me how before he left the West Coast in disgrace, he loaded the entirety of his long-aborning novel, that ceaselessly pullulating manuscript entitled *The Dizzies,* onto various ebook platforms. He artfully shattered and spliced the 2,333-page manuscript into nearly a *hundred thousand* parts, some as short as a sentence and others fifteen pages long. So that now, whenever someone buys a book on the Kindle, or any other e-reader, bits of *The Dizzies* meld seamlessly into the legitimate story. Each experience is unique, molded by reader response. The thing works, he said, like a dream.

Like *his* dream.

≈

I didn't believe him, but of course I did. I thought of how much I liked those pages of his unfinished novel that I'd read, all those years ago. Oh, how Professor Stoops had praised him in class! Sensibilism and Mood Writing and everything in between! Rolph had smuggled his life's work into the Kindle, in a form that fulfilled his goals completely. Granny-glassed pundits were bitching about the Kindle being the death of book culture, but no one was thinking about how to exploit it in the name of *beauty*.

"When will this all start?"

"It's already started," Rolph said, as his image wobbled and quit.

Now every book was his, from the Bible to *Invisible Man* to *The Remains of the Day*. I lost him, tried to Skype him back: nothing. It was entirely possible, I realized, that the diner didn't exist, at least not in Fort Greene. Rolph could have been calling from anywhere—Vancouver, Topeka, Hong Kong. Maybe his rant was all prerecorded. He was too smart to leave a trace, and I knew I would never hear from him again. Or rather, I would. I ordered a Kindle, loaded it with novels: *The Age of Innocence, Gone with the Wind, A Handful of Dust*. Every title burned with significance now. *Song of Solomon, Midnight's Children, Sophie's Choice*. Over the next few months, I read them back to back with strange excitement, unsure where the original stories ended and Rolph's began. I wondered when to tell everyone what it was, exactly, that they were reading.

SLIDE TO UNLOCK

You cycle through your passwords. They tell the secret story. What's most important to you, the things you think can't be deciphered. Words and numbers stored in the lining of your heart.

Your daughter's name.

Your daughter's name backward.

Your daughter's name backward plus the year of her birth.

Your daughter's name backward plus the last two digits of the year of her birth.

Your daughter's name backward plus the current year.

They keep changing. They blur in the brain. Every day you punch in three or four of these memory strings to access the home laptop, the work laptop. The email, the Facebook, the voicemail. Frequent-flier account. Every week, you're nudged to change at least one. You feel virtuous when the red security meter gets refreshed to green. You are safe.

Your hometown backward.

Your hometown plus the year you were born.

Your hometown backward plus the year you were born.

Olaffub72.

When you forget, they ask security questions, things only you would know. Mother's maiden name. First car, favorite color, elementary school.

First girl you kissed, that should be one.

Can these just be the passwords?

Stop stalling.

First time you had sex and did it count. Day, month, year. The full year or just the last two digits?

First concert you attended.

Name of hospital where you were born.

You wonder who writes these prompts. Someone has to write them.

Tip: Never use the same password for more than one account.

•

Last four digits of first phone number.

Last four digits of first work number.

Your daughter's best friend's name backward.

Your boss's first name.

Your first boss's last name plus the year you were born.

If you could remember and type out all your passwords, the entire hushed history of them, they would fill a book you could read in a minute. An abbreviated memoir, your life flashing before your eyes.

Last four digits of your cell, backward.

Favorite sports team?

Favorite sports team backward.

Serbas.

Pet's name.

Growing up, you knew a guy who had a dog named Serbas. You knew *two* guys with dogs named Serbas. They didn't like each other. The guys, that is. The dogs, who knows.

•

Guy's pet's name backward plus current year.

Favorite sibling, sibling who never let you down, plus last two digits of current year.

Mix of capitals and lowercase.

Six to eight characters long.

Ten to fourteen.

Stop stalling.

Mix of numerals and letters.

At least one symbol: #, %, *, !.

!

Father's hometown.

Mother's maiden name backward.

The girl at work you can't stop thinking of.

The girl at work plus current year.

The girl at work backward.

•

Ecinue.

The girl at work backward and lowercase plus last two digits of current year.

Passwords mean nothing to the machine. The machine lets you in to do what you need to do. It doesn't pass judgment. It doesn't care.

Your password appears as a row of dots.

Favorite film. But that keeps changing.

Vertigo. *Eraserhead*.

Favorite actor.

Actress who first made you hard, backward plus current year.

Best friend from high school.

Best friend from college.

Stop stalling.

Year you last saw your daughter.

Year you last saw your daughter plus her name.

•

There's a file on your work computer called "Passwords." But what if you forget the password to get into your work computer?

Her favorite toy. What she named her bike.

First girl you dated in college backward and lowercase.

Date of first death in the family.

Mother's name backward and year of her birth.

Year you finally started getting your shit together.

Year of First Communion plus name of priest.

Stop stalling.

Favorite author, backward and lowercase with middle letter capped for no reason save randomness.

Street address of the house you grew up in.

Sibling you don't talk to.

Spouse of sibling you don't talk to, who you text when you're drunk.

Stop stalling.

•

Your last name backward plus the day, month, year you find yourself at an ATM with a gun pressed between your shoulder blades, the gun in the hand of the guy who followed two steps behind after you swiped into the lobby, affecting a limp, the big guy who pretended to use another machine, then stepped behind you, quiet as a shadow, the big guy who already has your phone and wallet and the booze you thought it would be a good idea to run out and buy, at ten in the evening, your friend said she'd stay inside and you said you would hurry, but it was a good night for a walk, so while you're at it, out on your postprandial promenade, why not get some cash for the week to come?

The big guy with the very hard gun who is saying *Password* and *Right now* and *Stop stalling.*

AN ORAL HISTORY OF ATLANTIS

I HAVE SEEN *things I never wished to see, and every night I hear the ocean.* If it seems passing strange for a short man to sport such a lofty tone, consider that the other venues of pleasure are closed to me. I stand four foot eight in honest shoes—though hydraulic insoles and good posture get me to five even. I am allowed passage on most major roller coasters. Here at the lighthouse on the island's northern tip, I hang lanterns that mean "All Ports Closed" and spend my days pitched between anticipation and dissipation. I study the forgotten chapters of *The Chicago Manual of Style,* with their helpful instructions on bookbinding, perhaps included so that civilization can start anew, after the bomb or the wayward comet, when absolutely everything needs to be relearned.

That task may fall to me. I am compact but contain volumes. I know the lore of semaphore, the meaning of ship's bells, and the beautiful Beaufort scale, running from 0 to 12, with which I rate the force of wind. Right now we're at nil, *the sea is as a mirror.* I build drink after drink and wait for the rains to come.

My youth merits less than a sentence. We were immigrants. At eighteen, when it was clear nature would not begrudge another fraction of an inch, I stopped the height shakes, the protein packs, the kelp-based head balm that scented my sleep with sulfur and salt. My parents, those twin towers, proceeded to kick me out of the house, unconvinced to the end that I wasn't some prolonged sight gag.

"Hans," my father said, "it's time for you to fly."

Instead I walked—all the way to Manhattan, arriving at noon. This was the day before the day the city blew up every bridge, back when they thought rats spread the dread virus MtPR, pronounced "Metaphor," which they wanted to contain or exclude, it was hard to remember which. By one-thirty I had found gainful employment as a messenger, by quarter to four a studio apartment six stories above Water Street. Such is the dedication of the tiny. My room fronted a parking lot, a bit of suspicious real estate that never held a single car. Beyond stood a disused warehouse, ampersand and ampersand, all its signage washed away.

Summer became winter without a fall. Night classes, sit-ups, self-improvement. The room had come with a slightly slanted floor, a tin of ancient fruitcake, and a heavy box of books. In those pages, as frangible as potato chips, I read of miniature races the world over, and of entire cities that rise from the sea at times of grim conjunction. I took notes, and took notes on my notes.

There was a rod across the bathroom doorway. Every night, after my lucubrations, I snapped into a cunning pair of anklets and hung from it like some hairless bat god with a forbidden name full of diphthongs that would drive the pious insane just to say it. Thus I tried to touch the ground, dreamed my bones' slow migration.

One night, hanging insomniac, I felt light against my eyelids. Lamplight splashed through the window's grid, squaring my body in silver, as if ready for transfer to a larger canvas. My ears, flushed with cold night air, discerned a formidable rattle. It was three in the morning and somebody was typing with the window open, their hard strokes falling without a gap.

The mechanical music lulled me to sleep. When I awoke, snow covered my sill. The window across the lot was now closed. I studied the glass, but none of the dark shapes moved; below, the paving held no traffic. At two I went in search of lunch: a plate of chops as big as my torso, a glass of Ovaltine the size of my forearm, and a side of potatoes heavy as my brain. Then I ordered the same meal again.

At the other end of the counter sat a man of forty, tall but not disgustingly so, reading a foreign paper. He had most of his hair, gold wire glasses, and an intellectual slump to his thin frame. Whenever anyone coughed, he would wince, but then, so did everyone else. No one cared to contract Metaphor.

It was only when the man got up to leave that I recognized him as Walter Walter, the exiled Dutch writer. I had never heard of him before Water Street. One of his early books had been among those left in my apartment; I'd read it on a thunderstruck Halloween, as the walls went white with lightning and every terse phrase sent a chill. The library had his other titles: a few bracing *policiers* that established his name in criminous letters, plus a fat volume of memoirs with the demoralizing subtitle *The Early Years.* There had been some Low Countries scandal to run him out of Europe. So here he was, Walter Walter. His recent outpourings predicted more plagues and the rise of every atavism. The articles appeared in obscure journals of the occult persuasion, some of which I'd found neatly twined at curbside, next to self-published tomes on voodoo and hypnosis. Now I began to wonder if he lived in the area, if perhaps I had been reading his trash. I decided to follow Walter Walter.

I made my last pass at the spuds, left a quarter tip, and walked outside. The street was empty. One block east marched a conceivably Walteroid figure. The thickening snow made him look even thinner, as if primed to slip away between dimensions.

A crab of newsprint scuttled past. Every so often I'd sneak behind a bus shelter or trash can, not that he ever looked back. He turned left where I would normally turn left, then right where I'd turn right: Water Street. He dashed up the warehouse stairs. I stood by the lamppost as though plucked from a dream, studying the silent door. Later in my room, waiting for him to appear, I eased myself into his later essays. It was writing as disease—a torrent of speculation and data, with no trace of the proportion or wit that marked his admirable detective fiction. The only thing that had carried over was the fear.

Around five, I thought I could hear typing again, at a slower clip, the machine's report larded with silences. The sound stopped two hours later. Night had fallen, and with it the snow. I donned my foul-weather costume and nearly tobogganed down the stairs. I emerged to see Walter Walter, in derby hat and overcoat, heading north.

I kept a full block behind. Even if he slipped from sight, there were fresh tracks to be read. I counted ten cross streets, then stopped counting. The snow fell harder and the wind moved higher up the Beaufort scale. We went west, a tall man and his shadow incarnate, hitting a region of flashing lights and mechanical pleasures. Every lurid satisfaction could be had. I began to think less of Walter Walter, not that a sleuthing lilliputian should judge.

The lights, the falling snow, the Pine-Sol reek of every slippery venue—it was Christmas Eve, I realized. Good God, what had I become? Even a minikin should have standards. The dingy marquees and tattered banners touted assorted sordid scenarios, but in the most oblique possible terms. What did they mean by JAPANESE EGGPLANTS, SITTING PRETTY, BULBS WHILE-U-WAIT? I couldn't imagine—but of course I could. Or was I just seeing what I wanted to see?

My quarry finally ducked into the Wandering Womb, the initials like mammaries. A little bell rang; I heard him stamp his feet. The blacked-out windows bore slopes of steam. I counted thirty Mississippi before following.

It was a gaslit room, diverging from the straight exterior walls to curve like a ship, with a plush green carpet and bespoke lowboys and a player piano doing "The Salt-Water Rag." The walls were papered in velveteen, incised with anchors and fleurs-de-lis. At the antique cash register stood an even more antiquated man. The clerk wore a trig dark suit with a batwing collar and a cap that suggested a telegraph operator. I exchanged a ten, all I had, for a cup of brass slugs. They were heavier and smaller than quarters, with double W's raised on each face.

Eight booths were set into the walls, a narrow staircase suggesting more underground. I kept to the surface. The doors were mahogany with black curtains behind, some with boot tops beneath the fringe. Quaint signs said FRESH and HOT and WET. I could feel the clerk's eyes on me, so I ducked into Booth 3, marked THE ADMIRAL, and shut out the world. It smelled of paraffin and hearts of palm. In the dark I could make out a weathered hand crank and the stout shaft where the images lived, lunging up like a friendly seal. The bench was far too low, but a few stacked phone books made it an adequate perch: I was sitting atop all of Manhattan. Fitting a slug in the slot and my face to the eyepiece, I took a deep breath and manned the crank.

Somewhere in the shaft a bulb hummed on. It was like light from the nineteenth century, unsure and shrouded. A few dark cards clacked by in sequence, connected to the turning spindle. They were ink black, save the worn auroras at the corners. I spun faster, till the shadows gave up a shape.

But it wasn't a woman at all. It was a whale.

That tongue of a body barreled toward me, voluptuous tail held aloft. The white fins fanned in tandem. I turned, harder. Each image was stereoptically doubled, enabling an antediluvian 3D. I gasped as it corkscrewed, the crank damp; then the picture froze. Before the bulb could simmer, I entered another slug. A new set of cards came into play, whirring like wingbeats as I spun. The humpback rose and rose, through leagues of sepia, its body caught in reticulations of light as sun met sea. It was coming up for air, while I merged with that ancient water.

The whale, my whale, largely traveled alone. For a time it joined a regiment of dolphins, and periodically cut through schools of smaller fry, dagger-shaped, which parted like a veil around it. My mind supplied a plot where of course none belonged, some briny threnody with unseen hovering harpoons, *Moby-Dick* from the beast's point of view. I didn't believe it myself when I began to cry, my tears dripping off the glass onto the quick-milling cards: fresh, hot, and wet. I spun and blubbered, wondering what "Dutch treat" Walter Walter had come here to watch—whether the Wandering Womb was all whales, all the time, or if it offered deep-sea coelacanths, manatee matinees, self-propelled versions of the kraken.

The wind from the cards cooled my cheek, and I swear I felt a spray. To complete the cetacean sensations, a medley of bovine moans and expressive hinges, perhaps etched on a wax cylinder, issued from a cabinet by my legs. Sometimes the view straddled the waterline, whitecaps like flame; other times it looked shot from a boat, as a pod of humpbacks turned in sequence like the coils of a single vast serpent. But mostly things stayed underwater. My breathing adapted. Each slug seemed to last longer. The humpbacks sang in half-hour arias; my face was moist with sweat or spume. I woke when I started dreaming that the crank was an oar. The captain's command to fire was a klaxon blast from the front desk.

I emerged at four bells, the last one out. I tried asking the clerk about what I'd seen, but he just glared at the grandfather clock and smoothed his blond handlebars. I glimpsed myself in a pier glass, looking suitably depraved, with all the starch gone out of my shirt and the corners of my eyes as red as roses. Now it was a thousand blocks in the punishing snow. There were no footsteps to follow—the trail gone literally cold. As I turned onto Water Street, something glinted under the streetlamp: a pair of wire spectacles, like a crumpled insect, the lenses shivered in the snow. I put them on the handrail, where nobody could miss them.

≈

I never saw Walter Walter again. I lost him in the chaos, as the city heaved under the reign of Metaphor. People acted out, walking pie-eyed in the middle of traffic, playing musical instruments they had no right even owning. All the dogs died; electricity was touch and go. There were fewer rats since the bridges went, it was true; but the ones that remained had developed small nubs above the eyes, like primitive antennae.

At night I'd float in my tub, head against the enamel. I could hear elevators plumb and launch, wind howling through the garbage chute, ghostly voices of tenants too tall to talk to. It was a direct line into hidden nerves, a blueprint's subconscious filtered right through my skull, and it sounded like nothing so much as whalesong.

These private oracles served as a fix, but I passed my days in a benthic haze: I wanted to swim again, to be by my blowhole familiar. Unable to resist, abject as any addict, I finally made a return visit uptown, but the entire district had been rezoned; the mayor, linking Metaphor to vice, had decreed that only pizza parlors could operate there now.

Though you could find every kind of pepperoni, the Wandering Womb had wandered away. The pizzamongers all wore clip-on neckties and couldn't answer my questions. I was hungry, but I didn't stop. All the way home my mouth was open, and snowflakes fell in like krill.

I was seasick, although not from fantasy. The bridges, it seemed, had acted like stays securing Manhattan, and now it was moving south to freedom, while its edges slipped into anonymity. No more West Side Highway; no more FDR. And beginning that night, no more warehouse. An eraser-pink crane deleted it by a floor a day. As each level went, I could see nothing of human life but thousands of sheets of paper, perhaps all of Walter Walter's hopeless writing, whirling like birds as they blew away.

The epidemiologists, at wit's end, suggested taking up smoking, laughing more. I knew from my reading that my time drew near: throughout history, the little man has always been a convenient scapegoat. So before the mayor could megaphone any anti-nanist propaganda, I threw out all my books and climbed as far north as the Manhattoes allowed.

Here I see no one, I plan for the flood, I do my mundane midget things. Some nights the hour advances in step with the Beaufort scale, so that at seven *whole trees sway;* at nine *shingles may blow away.* I could chart other events for you: the Mylar hearts lost at the zoo, the gulls turning in wide circles like a planetary system. On the water to my left, on the water to my right float barges so big they're like pieces of the city, whole blocks wrenched loose with not a soul on deck. They continue at night, maybe the same ships in a hell of repetition. Their lights are orange and imploring, and glide in a line as steady as math: torches on some river whose name we've forgotten, whose name we were maybe never even meant to know.

ACKNOWLEDGMENTS

Thank you to PJ Mark and Andy Ward, and to the mighty Marni Folkman, Julia Harrison, Jaylen Lopez, Carrie Neill, Alison Rich, and the rest of the Random House team.

Most of these stories debuted at readings all around New York, and I'm grateful to folks who asked me to stand and deliver; to editors of publications where some of these fictions later landed; and to family members and fellow travelers over the last quarter century and change: Rachel Aviv, Tom Beller, Chris Brown, James Browning, Dusty Clayton, Sloane Crosley, Willing Davidson, Windy Dorresteyn, Andrew Eisenman, First Person Plural, Sam Frank, Manuel Gonzales, David Gordon, Gavin Grant, Lev Grossman, Nicole Haroutunian, Matt Higgins, Samantha Hunt, Joshua Jelly-Shapiro, J. Nicole Jones, the late Paul La Farge, Jane and Andy Lee, Tien-Yi Lee, Gillian Linden, Kelly Link, Yiyun Li, Veronica Liu, Sarah Manguso, JW McCormack, Michael Miller (whose invitations to read at *Bookforum* events nudged a trio of these tales into being); Aileen, S.K., and Yonzi Park; Ben Samuel, Janna Shaftan, Rebecca Shapiro, cover genius Will Staehle, Eugene Stein, Bonnie Thompson, Shawn Vestal, Ryan Walsh, Joanna Yas, James Yeh, Jane Yeh, Ray Ying, and Paul Yu.

ABOUT THE AUTHOR

ED PARK is the author of the novels *Same Bed Different Dreams* (2023), which was a finalist for the Pulitzer Prize and won the *Los Angeles Times* Book Prize for Fiction, and *Personal Days,* a finalist for the PEN/Hemingway Award. His short fiction has appeared in *The New Yorker, McSweeney's, The Baffler,* and other periodicals and anthologies, and he writes regularly for *The New York Review of Books, Harper's, Bookforum,* and elsewhere. Park was a founding editor of *The Believer* and a literary editor of the *Voice Literary Supplement* and has also worked in publishing. Born in Buffalo, New York, he lives in Manhattan with his family and currently teaches writing at Princeton University.

ABOUT THE TYPE

This book was set in Dante, a typeface designed by Giovanni Mardersteig (1892–1977). Conceived as a private type for the Officina Bodoni in Verona, Italy, Dante was originally cut only for hand composition by Charles Malin, the famous Parisian punch cutter, between 1946 and 1952. Its first use was in an edition of Boccaccio's *Trattatello in laude di Dante* that appeared in 1954. The Monotype Corporation's version of Dante followed in 1957. Though modeled on the Aldine type used for Pietro Cardinal Bembo's treatise *De Aetna* in 1495, Dante is a thoroughly modern interpretation of that venerable face.